MONSTER HIGH

FRIGHTS, CAMERA, ACTION! ™

THE JUNIOR NOVEL

ADAPTED BY
PERDITA FINN

BASED ON THE
SCREENPLAY WRITTEN BY
AUDU PADEN & **DAN SERAFIN**

Ⓛ Ⓑ
LITTLE, BROWN AND COMPANY
New York   Boston

MONSTERS, CAMERA, ACTION!

DRACULAURA

She wants to locate the magical Vampire's Heart—it will tell her who is the real queen of the vampires. She needs to set out on a monster mission!

CLAWDEEN WOLF

This wolf never abandons her pack, so she doesn't hesitate to lend a claw to Draculaura.

CLAWDIA WOLF

She studies creative writing in Londoom. When her sister Clawdeen and her ghoulfriends get there, she signs up for the adventure too. She wants to write about it!

ROBECCA STEAM

Without even knowing it, she keeps a secret in her heart. She gets her rocket boots in gear to help Draculaura.

HOODUDE VOODOO

Stitch by stitch, Hoodude will help Draculaura and her ghoulfriends.

CLEO DE NILE

The royal Cleo also signs up to search for the authentic queen of the vampires.

VIPERINE GORGON

This ghoul is Veronica von Vamp's makeup artist who met Draculaura and her ghoulfriends in Hauntlywood. She decides to pencil herself into their adventure!

VERONICA VON VAMP

The famous boo-vie actress has a lot to say, on and off the big screen.

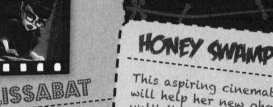

HONEY SWAMP

This aspiring cinematographer will help her new ghoulfriends until the credits roll THE END.

ELISSABAT

She is the true queen of the vampires. No one knows where she is, and Draculaura is determined to find her.

YGOR

This hunchback monster is Lord Stoker's helper. He would love to see a vampire boo-vie, even though he knows his master will never permit it.

LORD STOKER

The current leader of the vampires, at least until they find the new vampire queen. He is not ready t...

OPENING FRIGHT

C louds hid the sun. Mist swirled. A giant beast was running through the deserted streets. Horns sprouted from his head. Thick muscles bulged from beneath his hairy body. He had a gold ring in his nose. He was headed toward the local cinema! He snorted as he galloped past a skeleton slumped in the box office. He charged through the lobby and burst through the doors of the boo-vie theater.

Manny Taur was late again!

This jock of a Minotaur had almost missed the opening show of this year's hottest vampire movie. Everyone was there! All the glamorous ghouls and freaky frights from Monster High were settled in with popcorn. This was the big event. Everyone had been talking about it for weeks because no one wanted to miss a horror movie about one of their own. So many films got it wrong, but this boo-vie's stars were real-life creature features.

Monsters turned to glare at Manny as he panted in

the back of the room, trying to catch his breath. His huge chest heaved under his red T-shirt. Clawdeen and her werewolf brother, Clawd, growled at him to be quiet. Cleo de Nile and her boyfriend, Deuce Gorgon, grumbled as he squeezed in front of them toward an empty seat.

"Sorry, sorry," mumbled Manny Taur. "Coming through."

He stepped on Ghoulia Yelps's foot and she moaned.

"Shh!" demanded the monsters.

Only Draculaura, the sweetest vegetarian vampire at Monster High, didn't notice the intrusion of Manny Taur. Her eyes were glued to the screen.

A stunning star was descending the winding stairs of an ancient, crumbling castle. Veronica von Vamp commanded the screen. The movie was in black and white except for her lips; they were bloodred. She parted them as she sighed dramatically. She touched her forehead with her hand. "Oooh, I am not brave enough to be your queen, but the Heart tells me I must!"

Draculaura shook her head with disgust. She was not impressed with this performance.

At all. She shifted in her seat and watched the boo-vie star proclaim her love for a blond-haired hunk of vampire named Alucard.

"I am afraid to claim my throne," Veronica von Vamp overacted, "but I am not afraid to reveal my affections for you. Well, one of you."

Another vampire hottie lit up the screen. His hair was dark. The teenage ghouls in the audience oohed and aahed.

"Be with me, Princess, and my chiseled chin. Not Edweird!" commanded the blond vampire.

Edweird, the swarthy vamp, pushed Alucard aside. "No, Princess, forget Alucard! Be with me and my dazzling dimples!"

Maids dusting cobwebs in the castle swooned as they watched this fang-tastic rivalry.

"Her Majesty and Alucard will make such a regal couple," one maid gushed. Murmurs of agreement spread throughout the audience.

"Try dusting your eyes," said the other maid. "Edweird is the clear choice for her."

"Ooh!" Toralei purred from her seat in the movie theater. "Look at Edweird. Love the dimples!"

"Naw," Howleen disagreed with her. "I love Alucard's chin."

In the movie, Veronica von Vamp couldn't decide which horrifying hottie she preferred. In dramatic despair, she moaned again, batting her thick lashes. "If they could only see that there is more to me than beauty and royal destiny."

Draculaura was seething. She hated this movie.

"But, alas! I have a secret!" cried the actress. "I am not the ghoul you think I am!"

"Vampire scaritage requires you to reveal all of your secrets before your coronation as queen," Alucard reminded her.

"OH MY GHOUL!" shouted Draculaura, no longer able to contain herself. The usually mild-mannered vampire leaped up and began shouting at the figures on the screen. "Totes fake! Vampire royalty has no such rule!"

Her friends tried to get her to calm down. Robecca pulled on her arm. Hoodude, the voodoo doll, made shushing noises. Even Frankie Stein wanted her to be quiet. Draculaura was the only one not enjoying the boo-vie.

"Hey, sit down!" boomed Manny Taur. "Trying to watch a mmmmooooovvie here!"

Heath Burns agreed as his head burst into flames. "Stop blocking my view of Veronica von Vamp! She's hot!"

Hoodude whispered to Draculaura. "This is the best boo-vie ever. And Veronica von Vamp as the queen? Fangtastic!"

"Puh-lease!" exclaimed Draculaura. "She is a disgrace to vampire scaritage. Hauntlywood got it all wrong!" She was shouting now, and everyone was annoyed. They wanted to find out who Veronica von Vamp was going to choose—Edweird or Alucard.

"Shh!"

"Quiet!"

"Sit down!"

"Well, so-rry!" said Draculaura, not sorry at all and still not sitting down. After all, the reason they all went to Monster High was so they could study one another's scaritages and bring greater understanding about monsters to the whole world. This movie was no help at all as far as Draculaura was concerned. It was going to set vampire tolerance back eons. Draculaura began lecturing her classmates in the audience while the movie rolled on behind her. "I know how this really works. I was there! At Dracula's castle. Did you know vampires haven't had a proper queen for more than four hundred years?"

"SHHHHHHHHH!" the monsters screeched and screamed and howled. "SHHHHHHHHHHH!"

But Draculaura couldn't calm herself down. "THIS IS TOTALLY FAKE!"

The monster teens exploded, throwing popcorn and candy at her and shouting at her to sit down.

Draculaura stormed out of the theater. As she passed, Manny Taur mooed a sigh of relief. At least now nobody was going to remember him disrupting the boo-vie by coming late!

CHAPTER 2

MEAN GHOULS

D raculaura seethed in the boo-vie theater lobby while she waited for her friends. A sweet ghoul with long black hair highlighted in cherry pink, she hated making a fuss. Still, the history of the vampire queen was so important. She had really hoped the boo-vie would bring this issue into the public eye.

But now everyone was angry with her.

"Thanks for talking the whole time!" said Manny Taur, plowing past her after the movie ended.

Catty as ever, Toralei couldn't help making a snide comment. "Make way…it's Her Royal Fakeness!"

Howleen, her punk pink hair glowing brighter than ever, was just plain irritated. "Draculaura, you owe me a movie."

Poor Draculaura! She was embarrassed, but when she tried to explain herself, she just made matters worse. "Sorry if I got carried away," she apologized. "But that Veronica. She just frosts my fangs."

Her good friend Lagoona Blue shook her scales.

"You'd better get used to her. The Vampire Majesty boo-vies are the most popular ever made."

"Popular does not mean good," insisted Draculaura. She wasn't going to drop this. She couldn't. It was a matter of pride in her scaritage.

Hoodude swooned over an enormous cardboard poster of Veronica von Vamp. "Well, I loved it! And her!" He gave the photo of the boo-vie star a sloppy kiss.

All the ghouls laughed. But not Draculaura. "The real story is so much more fangtastic. I should know. I did grow up in Transylvania. At the royal vampire court. We don't usually talk about it. Had to leave in a hurry."

Robecca Steam stopped in her tracks, her gears and gadgets jangling. She was thinking about something that Draculaura had said during the boo-vie. "How is it," she asked, "that there hasn't been a vampire queen for four hundred years?"

"Yeah," chimed in Frankie. "Tell us all the voltageous details."

"Especially the romantic parts!" added Hoodude, tagging along behind the ghouls as they left the theater.

Her friends' curiosity helped Draculaura feel a little better. "Well, after the last queen's reign ended, the search began for the next ghoul in line."

"I love this!" Hoodude could be such a goof sometimes.

Draculaura continued. "They used an ancient jewel, 'The Vampire's Heart,' which was supposed to magically lead the way to the future queen. The search has gone on for four hundred years, but they still haven't found her."

Clawdeen stopped walking. "So the queen could be *anybody*?"

"And *anywhere*?" said Lagoona, stunned.

All of Draculaura's friends gathered around her. What a story she had to tell!

"Yep," said Draculaura. "Now wouldn't that make a better boo-vie?"

"I'll say!" said Hoodude. In his excitement, Hoodude tripped on the curb and accidentally zapped Heath with his volatile voodoo powers.

"Yeeowwch!" screamed Heath.

"Sorry, Heath," apologized Hoodude. "I still can't control my voodoo powers."

The teens had reached the front gates of Monster High. It was after dark and time for classes to begin. The bell tower chimed, announcing first period.

Hoodude stumbled closer to Draculaura. "Maybe you're secretly the queen!" he said to her.

"Wow!"

"Cool!"

"Claw-some!"

All the kids who had been making fun of Draculaura a little while ago looked at her in a whole new moonlight. Her werewolf boyfriend wrapped an arm around her. "Whoa!" he said in his low growl. "Clawd Wolf, dating royalty!"

Draculaura blushed.

"Allow me, Your Royal Highness," said Clawd, making a big show of holding open the front door to the school.

Frankie Stein rushed forward, getting into the spirit of it all. "Would you prefer the diamond or the gold crown, my queen?" She held out an imaginary jewel box.

Draculaura giggled. "Come on, Frankie, I think I'd know if I were really the queen." But she couldn't resist the fun. "I choose diamonds! They go with everything!"

Hoodude, who still had his popcorn box from the movie, held it up to his mouth like a megaphone. He yelled into it as the group of friends headed down the hallway. "Hear ye! Hear ye! Make way for Queen Draculaura!"

Monsters grabbing their books from their coffin-shaped lockers stared. They were still annoyed at the fuss Draculaura had made during the boo-vie. Draculaura felt embarrassed again.

Clawd headed off to the Creepateria. "I'll text you!"

"Bye!"

"Bye!"

"See you at Mad Science class!" said Frankie Stein, hurrying down the hall.

Draculaura stepped up to her locker, but before she could open it, Gory Fangtel and two of her sinister sidekicks appeared.

"Puh-lease, you the queen? You don't even have your vampire powers yet," sneered Gory. Gory was a super chic vamp with angled bangs, pointed ears, and teeth like razors.

Draculaura withered under her cold stare. "I...I... never said..."

Toralei and her cool cats, Purrsephone and Meowlody, joined the taunting of Draculaura. "You think you're all bat, but what have you ever done? *Meow!*"

The ghouls laughed meanly but stopped when they saw Frankie and Clawdeen approaching. There was

nothing those cats hated more than that werewolf girl.

"You'd better watch your fangs!" Clawdeen warned Gory Fangtel.

Lagoona Blue wrapped a shimmery arm around Draculaura. "Don't fret, love. It's what *you* think that's important."

Cleo de Nile sauntered over. "Do you want me to unleash a plague on them?" she asked Draculaura, raising one perfectly plucked eyebrow. "Because I have a new amulet that I've been dying to try out."

The mean monsters took a step back. Everyone was scared of Cleo...even her friends.

"Thanks, ghouls," said Draculaura meekly. "But...I...can fight my own battles."

"You'll be queen when trolls fly!" Gory laughed, and with that she turned into a bat and swooped down the hallway to class.

Toralei hissed at Draculaura before she too sauntered away with her friends.

Draculaura slumped against her locker. She was upset. "They're right." She sighed. "I have never done anything important. That's why I don't have all my vampire powers yet."

"What do you mean?" asked Lagoona Blue.

"Gory got hers a couple of hundred years ago

by saving a vampire lord from a sunburn. SPF, like, a thousand. I haven't done anything close to that. I may never get my powers."

Draculaura's friends crowded around. They knew how special she was—but how could they help Draculaura to realize that?

"You have something amazing in you," said Robecca. "I feel it—in here." The beautiful girl with the steampunk style touched her own heart. She wasn't making this up to help Draculaura feel better. She could really feel something glowing within her when she was close to her friend. Draculaura really was special. "You are going to surprise everyone."

"I hope. Thanks, Robecca."

But Draculaura still didn't have much faith in herself. What could she possibly do to gain real vampire powers?

CHAPTER 3

LORD STOKER'S TERRORTORY

A swarm of bats swooped past the turrets of an ancient castle on a hill. A lone wolf howled. Lightning flashed across the sky. It was an ordinary night in Transylvania at the ancestral home of Dracula.

In a study filled with books, a distinguished man with slicked-back hair was looking out the window at the storm. Worry lines creased his forehead. Lord Stoker turned as the heavy wooden door to his study was thrown open and a squat servant heaved himself into the room on short, fat legs.

"Master," panted Ygor. "The Royal Court of Vampire Dignitaries seeks audience with you at once."

A sinister smile lit up Lord Stoker's face. "Very well."

Ygor staggered over to the windows and threw

them open. A
cascade of bats
swooped into the
room, emitting
high-pitched squeals. *Eek! Eek! Eek!*

"What seems to be the problem?" said Lord Stoker,
addressing them directly.

One by one, each of the bats transformed into a
vampire. They were well-dressed officials with medals
and ribbons.

"Lord Stoker, we demand to know how the search
for the queen is going!" said the first dignitary.

Lord Stoker arranged a pleasant-looking expression
on his face like a mask. "Well—" he began.

"You've had four hundred years!" interrupted
another of the dignitaries. "Where is she? We think
you are enjoying your temporary role as our leader
much too much!"

Lord Stoker drew himself up to his full height and
glared at the assembled vampires. "I assure you that
I have everything under control. The search for the
queen—"

But the vampires had been hearing this for
centuries. They were fed up. "This is taking too long!"
shouted a vampire. "We need a true leader. Vampires
are forgetting their scaritage."

"We just heard that Vampire Prep, our most

prestigious vampire academy, is on the verge of closing!" chimed in another vampire.

With a stern look, the oldest of the dignitaries stared at Lord Stoker. It was time to issue the edict. "The Vampire Court has voted. If you do not find a new queen by the end of the week, you will be fired."

Lord Stoker steadied himself against his enormous oak desk. He spluttered as he tried to collect himself. "Eh…eh…" he said. "Well…you are in luck."

The dignitaries cast cold vampire eyes on him.

"Because…because…" Lord Stoker improvised. "I…I…"

The dignitaries exchanged suspicious glances.

"I already found the queen!" blurted out Lord Stoker.

Ygor scratched his almost-bald head. This was news to him.

"Really?" The vampire dignitaries were startled. "Really?"

"Really?" muttered Ygor, joining in.

Lord Stoker was an expert liar. "Yes! I used the Vampire's Heart and, why, just today, I found her. Isn't that right, Ygor?"

Ygor looked confused. "No, no, you lost the Vampire's Heart when—Owww!"

Lord Stoker had squashed his boot down on top of Ygor's foot. He smiled charmingly at the dignitaries.

Ygor tried to wriggle loose but he couldn't. "Ygor means yes, Master. Yes. Oooh! Oooh! Oooh! Yes! Yes! Yes!" What did he have to say to get Lord Stoker to let him go? "In fact, her coronation is next week!"

Lord Stoker lifted his foot and Ygor breathed a huge sigh of relief. He gave Lord Stoker a thumbs-up sign.

In their excitement, all the dignitaries turned back into bats. They began flying around the study. "Eek! Eek! Eek!" At last they would have a queen again! Four hundred years was a long time, even for the undead. "Queen! Queen! Queen!" they said in their high-pitched squeals.

Just as he flew out of the window into the storm, one of the bats turned back to Lord Stoker. "Good. We meet the queen next week, Stoker."

"Or it's daylight for you!" added one of the other dignitaries. With that final warning, they screeched back into the night. Lord Stoker watched as they flew into the clouds.

As soon as he was sure they were gone, he turned on his servant. "Next week?! Ygor, have you lost your mind?!"

Ygor looked dumbfounded. Of course he hadn't lost his mind. He pulled a container out of his pocket. "No, Ygor keeps it in this little jar."

Lord Stoker threw up his hands in frustration. Why did he have to do everything himself? He stormed out of the study, marching down a hallway filled with suits of dusty armor and paintings of long-forgotten vampire lords and ladies. He pulled open the doors to the throne room. Embroidered tapestries lined the walls. Candelabras covered in wax hung from the ceiling. Everything was covered in cobwebs. It had been a long time since he'd been in there. He stood and stared at the empty throne. What was he going to do? How could he possibly have a coronation? More important, how could he make sure that he remained in charge?

Ygor limped in behind him. "How are you going to find a queen in a week? Your niece stole the Vampire's Heart four hundred years ago when—"

Lord Stoker threw his hand over Ygor's mouth. Still, Ygor kept trying to talk.

Frustrated, Lord Stoker narrowed his eyes and spoke very slowly. "I don't want to find the queen."

"Right!" exclaimed Ygor. "Because…eh…" He stopped, puzzled again. "Remind Ygor why again, Master."

"Because once we have a queen, I will no longer be in charge."

"Aaaaah! Yes!" Ygor's round face broke into a smile.

"I am the only one who knows what's good for vampires," said Lord Stoker. He was pacing back and forth across the marble floor of the throne room. "What I need is a fake queen, one I can control and bend to my will."

"Yesss, Master!" agreed Ygor.

Lord Stoker looked up at the tapestry hanging on the wall. It showed the royal vampire kings and queens through the ages and all their descendants. What caught Lord Stoker's eye, however, was a very pretty ghoul with bangs and long hair streaked with pink. She wasn't particularly scary or all-powerful like a vampire king or queen. She was cute.

Lord Stoker cackled. "There! She's perfect! The daughter of Dracula with all of his so-called enlightened ideas about monster equality. I remember this girl from court." He studied the girl in the tapestry. There was an evil glint in his eye. He could be so diabolical! "She was always so naive, insecure, and feeble," he remembered. "I imagine she doesn't even have her vampire powers yet."

He addressed the girl in the tapestry. "You won't have the courage to question me. Isn't that right, my new queen?" He laughed.

Confused, Ygor began laughing too. "Ha-ha, yes," he said, not understanding the plan.

Thousands of miles away, across an ocean, across a continent, Draculaura had no idea what Lord Stoker was plotting.

CHAPTER 4

SUDDENLY ROYAL

raculaura's iCoffin was buzzing. It was her beloved father. She giggled as she talked to him on her way to class, smiling at Frankie Stein headed toward her in the hall.

"Okay, Daddy," agreed Draculaura. "I'll floss my fangs! And I'll call you in six months when you can come out again. Smooches. Love you!"

"Six months?" Frankie had only heard the tail end of the conversation. She shifted her books in her hands.

"Business trip to Antarctica," explained Draculaura. "You know, six months of daytime, then six months of night."

Toralei and her friends passed the girls in the hallway and bowed mockingly to Draculaura. "Oh, make way, make way," hissed Toralei. "It's Her Royal— *meow*—Fakeness!"

Toralei's friends snickered. Draculaura blushed. They just wouldn't drop it. It had been days now and they were still making fun of her. She dreaded having to endure their teasing in Mr. Rotter's class. Frankie smiled at her encouragingly, but it didn't make any difference. It was awful.

The moment she walked into the chamber, Gory Fangtel announced, "All hail Queen Draculaura!" Ghouls at their desks burst into laughter.

Draculaura tried to ignore them. She sat down at her seat next to Frankie. Thank goodness she had some friends to stick by her!

Mr. Rotter was fussing with a projector. He turned his green face around and glared at the ghouls making noise. "Settle down!" he whined. "Today we'll be continuing our discussion of history. This is your scaritage! The journey to the boo-world!"

He pulled down a film screen and clicked on the projector. While his back was turned, spitballs flew through the air and landed in Draculaura's hair. Frankie stared at Gory and Toralei, but it didn't make any difference.

Mr. Rotter pointed at a map projected onto the screen. "Londoom was a stopping point for immigrating monsters. They left their homelands for many reasons."

Toralei leaned forward in her seat. "Probably because they were an embarrassment to their kind."

"Or 'cause they made up stories about being queen." Gory snickered.

Draculaura sank down in her chair. She wished she were an invisible ghoul or a disappearing creature or with her father down in Antarctica. When Gory blew another spitball at her and it landed on her cheek, she exploded. She couldn't take it anymore. "Stop torturing me!" she yelled.

Mr. Rotter whirled around. "Draculaura!"

The ghoul gasped. She was usually so well behaved in class.

"Don't spook until you are spooken to!" said Mr. Rotter. "Detention!"

Gory and Toralei exchanged triumphant looks. Frankie just shook her head. She had no idea how to help her friend.

Draculaura moaned softly to herself. Could this day possibly get any worse?

Just at
that moment,
the intercom
began to
crackle and the
imperious voice of Headmistress Bloodgood filled the
classroom. "Attention, Draculaura, report to my office.
Immediately."

Well, at least it gave her an excuse to get out of
class—and away from Gory and Toralei. She gathered
up her books and whispered to Frankie, "Hashtag…in
trouble. Again."

Draculaura hurried through the empty corridors
to Headmistress Bloodgood's office. She hated being
in trouble. She'd never even had detention before.
Flustered, she burst into the office, already apologizing.
"I am so so so sorry I yelled in class, Headmistress.
I—"

Headmistress Bloodgood interrupted her.
"Draculaura, you are…"

Draculaura gasped with surprise—not at the
headmistress but at all the vampires and bats

assembled in the office. There were official vampire guards, and Ygor, and Lord Stoker himself. What could they possibly be doing here? Were they sending her back to Transylvania? Just for yelling in class?

"You are the next vampire queen," finished Headmistress Bloodgood. Thrilled, the headmistress removed her head with a flourish.

The guards bowed to her. Lord Stoker smiled at her. "You are the chosen one," he said smoothly.

Could this be true? Or was this some elaborate prank to make even more fun of her? "Lord Stoker? What are you doing here?" she asked, finding her voice.

"I was led to you." He smiled. "By the Vampire's Heart!"

Draculaura was speechless.

Lord Stoker brought forth an ornate jeweled box. He opened the heavy lid, and there, resting on a bed of crushed red velvet, was the famous gem. There was no mistaking it. It was the stuff of legends. Lord Stoker presented it to Draculaura

and she timidly rested her hand on the Vampire's Heart.

Draculaura looked at the glowing jewel beneath her hand in disbelief. How could this be?

"See how it glows in your presence?" said Lord Stoker. He quickly closed the box before anyone could study the jewel.

Draculaura was dumbfounded. "I really am the next queen." At her words, the vampire guards fell to their knees. Lord Stoker bowed.

"All hail the new vampire majesty!"

Just as the guards were saluting their new queen, a crowd of ghouls barged into the office, all talking at once. In the midst of all of Draculaura's best friends was Gory Fangtel—who clearly didn't want to be there. She was baring her fangs.

"Headmistress Bloodgood," said Frankie, talking

a mile a minute. "Gory has been picking on Draculaura all day and with…"

At the sound of Draculaura's name, all the vampires saluted again. "All hail the queen!"

"Thank you!" said Cleo de Nile, who naturally assumed they were addressing *her*. "That never gets old."

But Frankie, Robecca, Ghoulia, Clawdeen, and Lagoona noticed that everyone in the room was a vampire—and they were all on bended knees in front of Draculaura. Her friends stared at Draculaura in disbelief.

Draculaura blushed. "Um, they mean me. I'm the next vampire queen." But she said it as if she was trying to convince herself that it was true.

"Wow!" gushed Frankie, the bolts on her neck shooting out sparks.

"Claw-some," howled Clawdeen.

"Hooray!" said Robecca.

"Okay," said Cleo, more than a little surprised.

But the person who really couldn't believe it was Gory Fangtel. Her face was an ugly knot of rage. "Draculaura the queen?! No way!"

The vampire guards glared at her. Lord Stoker bared his teeth.

"Um…I mean, uh…no way…" stumbled Gory, trying to recover. "No way I won't be the first to say congrats! Have I told you how much I *loooove* that outfit, Your Majesty?"

But Draculaura wasn't falling for it. Besides, she was still in too much shock herself.

"We must leave for Transylvania immediately," Lord Stoker said briskly. The guards, used to obeying him, prepared to leave.

"But no!" said Draculaura frantically. It was hard enough to accept that she was queen, but she certainly wasn't ready to abandon her ordinary life. "I can't be queen. It would mean leaving all of my friends, and Monster High is my home. What if I never come back?" She whimpered softly at the very thought of it.

Gory made a gagging noise that she quickly covered up with a sweet smile.

Lord Stoker tried to hide his irritation. "Draculaura, listen to me," he began. "Yes, being queen is difficult for one of your...limited abilities. But you are important. Don't worry," he said, patting her on the head. "I will take care of all the messy details. The Heart chose you for a reason. It is for the good of your people."

Headmistress Bloodgood, her head in her hands, agreed.

Draculaura was overwhelmed. The room felt like it was spinning. "I am... important," she said to herself. Could it really be true?

"I've always said you were!" said Gory Fangtel, trying to suck up to the new queen.

Draculaura caught the eye of Frankie Stein, who smiled at her. Thank goodness her friends were here. What would she do without them in Transylvania? That's when it began to sink in. She was the queen. Why couldn't she bring her friends along? "Can my ghoulfriends come?" she asked Lord Stoker.

Clawdeen gave a low growl of excitement. "Oh, I've always wanted to see Transylvania!"

"Of course!" agreed Lord Stoker, eager to get away from Monster High before the headmistress began asking too many questions. "The queen needs her ladies-in-waiting to attend her at the coronation. Which is next week, so let's hurry it up."

Draculaura ran to the headmistress. "Please, please, can they come? Please? It would be deaducational!"

The headmistress was thrilled to have the vampire queen at her school and not at Vampire Prep. It sent such a strong message to the monster world after all. "I suppose it would be a good chance to learn about your monster scaritage in person. Okay!"

"Fangulous!" exclaimed Draculaura.

All the ghouls cheered with excitement. They were going to be traveling abroad!

"Yay!"

"Woo-hoo!"

"You go, Queen!" cheered Robecca.

Gory wrapped an arm around Frankie and Cleo. "All right! Yeah! Woo-hoo!"

"Sorry, Gory," said Cleo, removing Gory's arm. "You'll be at the vampire court *when trolls fly....*"

"I should have seen that coming," sneered Gory.

Lagoona Blue was checking her schedule on her iCoffin and looking disappointed. "Hate to be a

bummer," she apologized. "But Ghoulia, Frankie, and I have a major Clawculus project due next week."

Frankie gave Draculaura a big hug. "We are totes happy for you!"

Something about Frankie's embrace made the news real for Draculaura. She was going to be queen. She was going to wear a crown, and sit on a throne, and go to balls—and dance. "I have to tell Clawd!" she realized.

What would he think of all of this? She hoped he'd be excited to be dating a *real* vampire queen!

Clawd was bounding by the office when the ghouls called to him. At first he too worried that he'd gotten in trouble. "Did I bury something I wasn't supposed to?"

Draculaura pulled him aside and whispered into his ear. "Hey, sweetie. Remember how we joked about me being the vampire queen?"

"Right!" barked Clawd, ever cheerful. "That was hilarious!" He started chuckling, then noticed how Draculaura wasn't joining in. "You're not laughing."

Draculaura twisted the ends of her hair. "Yeah, well, it turns out"—she laughed nervously—"I kinda, sorta am the next vampire queen. And I have to leave for Transylvania. Like, now."

Clawd's face drooped. "So I guess that means we're...we'll be..."

"Yes, we'll be apart." Draculaura took Clawd's large, soft paw in her hand. "For seven days."

"That's like a...month in wolf time! Who will take me on walks?"

Draculaura began scratching Clawd behind his ears. His tongue lolled out of his mouth. "Oh, Clawd. You'll be fine. You're a good boy. Who ruvs you? Who does? I do!"

She pulled a ball out of her purse and Clawd barked with excitement. Draculaura tried to hold back her tears. "Now"—she sniffed—"fetch!" She threw the ball out the door and down the hall. Clawd looked lovingly at Draculaura, but then he whimpered as his wolf instincts took over. He ran as fast as he could after the ball, howling as he went.

Draculaura let out a sob as she watched him go.

"Come!" announced Stoker, tired of all of this. "We must leave at once. Your throne awaits!"

"Voltageous!" cheered Frankie.

"Claw-some!" whooped Clawdeen.

Draculaura took one last look around the halls of Monster High. Her life was about to completely change…forever.

As she headed toward the front entrance, ghouls and monsters came out of their classrooms to see if the rumors were true.

"What's happening?"

"What's going on?"

"Is Draculaura really the vampire queen?"

Word was spreading like wildfire. Hoodude couldn't believe it when he heard it, but when he saw the limousines parked out in front of the school, he decided it must be true.

"Wow!" said the ghouls.

"Oooh fancy," murmured Cleo. She liked traveling in style!

Draculaura turned back one last time toward the school. "Good-bye everyone! I'll see you at my coronation." She was openly crying now.

"Come on, ghoul!" said Clawdeen. "Your throne is waiting."

Increasingly impatient, Lord Stoker practically shoved the girls into the limousine and slammed the door behind them.

Draculaura peered out the window at the kids calling out congratulations to her. The engine started. Tears were pouring down her cheeks, and there was Clawd, the ball in his mouth, running toward the limos. He spat out the ball. "Good-bye, Draculaura," he howled. "Monster High will miss you! I'll miss you! AH-ROOOOOOOO! AH-ROOOOOOO! AH-ROOOOOO," he began howling.

But the limousines had already vanished down the road.

CHAPTER 5

NEXT STOP, TRANSYLVANIA

A train roared through dark forests and craggy mountains. It chugged past abandoned towns. It sped through fog-filled valleys and raced through tunnels blacker than night.

Inside the train, the ghouls were enjoying the lavish splendor of the royal compartments. There were velvet-tufted sofas and gold-framed oil paintings. The ghouls were doing their nails and claws and getting ready for their arrival at the castle.

Ygor entered with a servant, who was carrying a silver tray with goblets filled with a thick red liquid. Ygor bowed low before Draculaura. "Your, erm, tomato juice, Your Majesty." Everyone on the train had been surprised that the new vampire queen was a vegetarian.

"Thank you," said Draculaura, taking a sip of her drink.

Ygor glared at the servant. "Bow to the queen!"

"O-M-Ghoul." Draculaura giggled. "You don't have to do that."

"It's tradition," said Ygor, confused.

"As my dad always says, 'Traditions can change.'" Draculaura handed goblets to her friends.

Ygor was muttering to himself, clearly upset. "And as the master says, 'Traditions must never change and that traitor Dracula's ideas are—'" He stopped, realizing Draculaura was staring at him. "Uh…uh…uh…enjoy your juice!" He staggered out of the compartment with the servant.

Clawdeen leaned back against the soft pillows of the sofa. "So, tell us more about what it was like to grow up in the vampire court! All that history!"

Cleo snorted. "Sixteen hundred years of aristocracy is nothing to brag about. Egyptian royalty has shoe sales that last longer than that."

Draculaura clapped her hands. "Oh! The vampire court was totes amazing!" She pointed at one of the paintings on the wall that showed women in long gowns and men in floor-length capes dancing together. "The beautiful dresses! The grand balls! I used to sneak downstairs with my best friend Elissabat, Lord Stoker's niece, to watch the vampire waltz. We all had so much fun!" She giggled at the memory of it. "Well, except for old crankypants Stoker!"

Clawdeen studied the painting. She pointed at a sour-faced vampire lurking in the corner. "Yeah! Looks like he hasn't smiled in four hundred years."

"Stoker wanted control over all other types of monsters. The whole court was divided," explained Draculaura. She was really enjoying sharing her history. It was so much better than feeling frustrated watching that stupid movie with Veronica von Vamp that got everything wrong.

Robecca Steam brushed aside one of her dark curls. She was loving this adventure; it made her feel all warm and lit up inside. Besides, she had a deep connection to Transylvania, which she explained to the ghouls. "My father, Hexiciah Steam, arrived in Transylvania just before the 'great split,' when the more open-minded monsters emigrated to the Boo World."

Draculaura nodded. This was why her family had gone to Monster High. "Stoker and my dad did not get along," she gossiped. "You see, my dad's very best fiend was Lord Stoker's younger brother."

"So what happened to him?" asked Robecca. "Did he head off on a mysterious expedition and no one has ever heard from him since...or something like that?"

Draculaura's dark eyes widened with surprise. "Um, yeah. *Exactly* like that."

"Wow, good guess," said Clawdeen. She scratched at her ear with her just-manicured claws.

Robecca was looking out the window at the passing mountains. Something Draculaura had said reminded her of *something*—only she couldn't remember what it was. "I feel like I know this story."

Draculaura continued. "The one who disappeared? His only daughter was Elissabat, and she was put under her uncle Stoker's authority. There was a big argument between Stoker and my dad about her future. Poor Elissabat." Draculaura sighed. "She wanted to be an actress, but Stoker put his foot down. He said that she had to stay at the court as a vampire-in-waiting."

"So your dad helped her?" said Cleo.

"He tried!" said Draculaura. "But then she disappeared. Just before we fled Transylvania."

The brakes of the train screeched, the whistle blew, and the voice of a vampire conductor called out their impending arrival at Castle Dracool.

The girls peered out the window, eager for their first sight of the famous castle. From far away, in another car at the back of the train, came muffled screams and gasps of pain.

Something invisible was attacking Ygor in the baggage compartment. *Zap! Zap! Zap!* "Ouch!" screamed Ygor. He felt like he was being stuck with sharp pins, only he couldn't see anything. The train jostled and again Ygor was zapped and stung. He fled the car, looking for his master.

A sarcophagus fell from the luggage rack as the train rounded a corner—and out popped Hoodude! He was a stowaway! He'd been zapping Ygor with his out-of-control powers. "Whoa!" he said, lumbering over to the window and taking in the scenery. "Glamorous vampire court, here I come!" He looked over his stitches to make sure he didn't have any loose

threads. He wanted to look sharp—even
if he was patched together with rag-doll hair and
button eyes.

With a final wheeze, the train lurched to a stop.
More luggage tumbled out on Hoodude's head. *Crash.
Zap!* It was hard being a voodoo doll, that was for
sure, but at least he was in Transylvania with the other
ghouls.

Hoodude peeked out the window through the
steam from the train and the fog and saw the ghouls
standing on the platform with Lord Stoker and Ygor.
Looming over the station was the imposing presence of
Castle Dracool, with its turrets and drawbridges.

"Behold, Castle Dracool!" announced Lord Stoker
grandly.

"Oooh!"

"Ahhh!"

"Magnificent!"

"It's no pyramid," said Cleo drily. The steam and the fog were making her hair frizz.

Clawdeen was impressed. "It looks just like the one in the Vampire Majesty boo-vies."

Ygor's face crumpled. "Ygor's not allowed to see boo-vies," he said sadly.

"A vulgar waste of time," sneered Lord Stoker. He swirled his cape around him dramatically. "Blegh!"

Draculaura ignored old crankypants. She was too excited. "Ah! I haven't been here in for-evs! Such memories! C'mon, ghouls! I'll show you around!"

She linked arms with her friends and they all headed to the castle.

CHAPTER 6

DRESSED TO THRILL!

The wind was howling, the castle was creaking, and it was perfectly spookerific. The ghouls wanted to jump on every canopy bed and explore every secret passage. There were banquet halls and ballrooms, dressing rooms and cobweb-covered boudoirs.

Ygor followed the gaggle of ghouls. He was carrying their suitcases, traveling coffins, and mummy cases. With every step he took, he winced and moaned. It was like he was being stuck with needles again. What could it be? Inside a carry-on bag, Hoodude did his best to stay quiet.

"Oof," he gasped when Ygor tripped. It wasn't easy being a stowaway.

Draculaura wanted to visit the throne room first. Gold glinted from the sconces on the walls, from the candelabras, and from the throne itself at the very end of the room. Draculaura walked along the plush red carpet that led to the throne, picked up the bejeweled

crown that rested on the seat, put it on her head, and
sat down. She looked at her friends, trying to be as
regal as possible. But it was no use. Even with a crown
on her head in the vampire's throne room, she still just
felt like herself. She burst into giggles and her friends,
relieved, joined in.

Draculaura took off the crown and jumped up.
There was plenty of time to get serious about being
queen. Now she wanted to have fun. She went over to
the wall and began pulling on the sconces until she
found the one that wiggled. With a quick twist, the
entire wall began to move—and exposed a hidden
staircase. The ghouls ran inside and the wall closed
right behind them.

Up they climbed in the darkness until they
emerged through a giant fireplace into the Royal
Chambers. In the center of the room was a bed draped
in satin and velvet. Beautiful carpets covered the floor.
But Draculaura wasn't interested in any of this.

She threw open the closet door to reveal a room bigger than most department stores, filled with dresses and shoes and hats and gowns. There were black  corsets trimmed with silver braids and flounced silk skirts elaborate with ruffles. There were lace gloves and fishnet stockings embroidered with diamonds. If a fashion designer from the court of some old French king had gone to work at the most punked-out, ghoulish store at the Maul, this was what it might have looked like. Robecca picked up a blouse dripping with silver chains. Cleo admired a pair of black sandals with heels. Clawdeen wrapped herself in a fake-fur boa.

The girls giggled while they dressed themselves in finery.

But Draculaura was overwhelmed with feelings about being home. She went back into the bedchamber and looked out the window to the valley below. This was her kingdom now. Her. Kingdom. "Yay!" she said aloud. "Woohoo! I forgot how wonderful this castle is!"

"Amazing!" said Clawdeen, collapsing on the four-poster bed.

"So dark and dreary!" said Draculaura, joining her.

"I love it!" Robecca laughed breathlessly.

"Nice as far as castles go," admitted Cleo, admiring herself in the enormous mirror.

A knock on the door announced Ygor. "Lord Stoker has sent Ygor to bring the new queen to his study to hear the rules."

Draculaura bounced up from the bed. "Well, duty calls."

"Later!" said Clawdeen.

Robecca wished her good luck.

Cleo waved good-bye. "Queen problems, am I right, ladies?" she said.

The girls settled into the luxurious pillows on the bed. They were happy for their friend. Not only was she going to be a fangtastic queen of the vampires—they were going to love being her ghouls-in-waiting!

CHAPTER 7

THE TRUTH BITES

Draculaura followed Ygor through the twisting hallways of the castle to Lord Stoker's study.

"Wait in here, my queen," he instructed her. "Do not touch *anything*! Master gets very grumpy." He backed out of the room, bowing, but accidentally shut his hand into the door behind him as he was leaving. "*Ah-ouch!*" he wailed.

Draculaura looked around the book-filled room. She spun the globe. She picked up a skull and wondered whose it might have been. Bored, she sat down at Lord Stoker's desk and rocked back and forth in the leather chair. She glanced at the papers scattered over his desk, but they looked boring and serious. Absentmindedly, she pulled open one of the desk drawers and right there, not even in its special box, was the Vampire's Heart.

Draculaura gazed at it with wonder. This jewel had recognized her as queen. It really should be in a

place of honor, she thought. She leaned over to touch it. She wanted to see that magical glow again that had revealed who she really was.

But nothing happened.

She placed both of her hands on it. But it didn't glow. Curious, she took it out of the drawer and began examining it.

She didn't notice the coffin leaning up against the wall slowly beginning to open. Lord Stoker, his arms crossed over his chest, was opening his heavy-lidded eyes. "What are you doing?" he shrieked in horror.

"Aaaahhhhhh!" yelped Draculaura, totes surprised. "You ever heard of knocking? So rude…"

Lord Stoker lurched across the room and snatched the Heart out of Draculaura's hands. "What are you doing with that? You didn't find anything else, did you?" He glared at her suspiciously.

"I…I…just touched the Heart," said Draculaura.
Why was Lord Stoker acting so paranoid? "But it
didn't light up. Vampire scaritage says it always
glows when the true queen touches it. What gives?"

Lord Stoker twisted his red lips into a smile.
"No need to worry your pretty little head. I just
have to uh…uh…change the batteries and it…uh
oh." From the stunned expression on Draculaura's
face, he realized that he had revealed his secret.

"Batteries?!" gasped Draculaura. "Oh! My!
Ghoul! It's a fake!" She leaned back in the chair,
overwhelmed. "Wait, that means I'm not queen?"

Lord Stoker gave a nervous chuckle.

Draculaura shook her head. This really was a
nightmare. The bad kind. "The people need to be
told," she realized, as horrible as that would be.
She could just imagine what Toralei and Gory
would say when she went back to Monster High.
She would have to tell her friends. She got up to
go, but Lord Stoker whipped his cape across his
face and transformed into a bat. He swooped
toward the door, turned back into a vampire, and
blocked her from leaving.

"I command you! Stop!" he shouted at her. "What the people need is a queen. And you are just the ghoul for the job."

"Why me?" Draculaura asked. "Why not try to find the real queen?"

Lord Stoker studied the meek vampire girl in front of him. He had chosen well. "Because you will do as I say!" he ordered her. He drew himself up to full vampire height. "I will remain in charge, of course, and in return, you will live a life of luxury as the queen."

Draculaura crumpled into a chair.

"Not a bad deal," Lord Stoker said triumphantly.

"This isn't right," Draculaura said in a defeated voice.

Lord Stoker's black eyes glinted with mischief and cruelty. "Dear Draculaura, aren't you tired of monsters like—what was her name? Ah—that Gory picking on you? Don't you want to matter? To go down in history

as a famous, important vampire?" He paused
for a moment, waiting to strike the final blow. "Don't
you want to finally get your vampire powers?"

"Well, yes I do, but—"

"Good!" said Lord Stoker. "Then you shall serve as
my puppet. All you have to do is jump when I pull the
strings."

Thoughts were tumbling through Draculaura's
head. Surely she could convince Lord Stoker to let her
use her power to make a difference? As queen she'd be
able to help all kinds of monsters, wouldn't she? Would
that really be so bad? "What do you want me to do?"

"Your first order of business," Lord Stoker said
icily, "will be to stop the intermingling of vampires
and other monsters."

Draculaura gasped. This was against everything
her father believed in.

"You and I will turn back the clock to a time when
vampires ruled the world!" proclaimed Lord Stoker.
"There will be strict rules to ensure that we return

to our former glory as the most respected and feared monsters in the land. Do we have an agreement…my queen?"

At these words, Lord Stoker evaporated in a haze of black smoke and reappeared beside Draculaura's chair. She screamed at the top of her lungs.

"I don't think you have a choice," he threatened.

Draculaura looked up at Lord Stoker's sinister smile and burst into tears. She felt so completely helpless. Sobbing, she ran out of the room. She just had to get away from him.

Lord Stoker watched her flee and rubbed his hands together devilishly. Oh, this was all going just as he had planned!

CHAPTER 8

BAD SCARE DAY

And that's reason number one hundred and four why pyramids are superior to castles. Reason number one hundred and five—"

Clawdeen yawned, interrupting Cleo.

The ghouls had gone exploring to the kitchens to find snacks and were returning to the royal chambers when they heard sobbing. They flung open the door, but no one was there. The cries were coming from the closet.

Sitting on a pile of shoes and scarves was Draculaura.

At the sight of her friend so upset, Robecca felt like her heart might break.

"What's wrong?" asked Clawdeen.

Draculaura wiped away her tears. "Nothing," she tried to say. But it was no good. She couldn't keep a secret from her beasties. She started sobbing again. "Except that I'm not the real queen!"

The ghouls looked at each other, confused.

"But...the Vampire's Heart," Robecca said. "At Monster High when you touched it, it glowed. You're the queen."

Draculaura heaved with sobs as she tried to explain. "Lord Stoker faked it!" she wailed. "The real one is gone. And Stoker chose me to be the queen because I'm just a nobody who will do whatever he says."

Cleo noticed a pretty little dress in the closet. "You still get all of these clothes, though, right?" The other ghouls glared at her. "I mean, being a fake queen is still better than not being royal at all."

Clawdeen sat down next to Draculaura. "Never thought I'd say this, but Cleo has a point: The vampires have been without a queen for a long time. You'd still be helping."

"No!" wailed Draculaura. "He wants me to make vampires rule over all other monsters! We won't be allowed to be friends with anyone but vampires."

"That's horrible!" said
Clawdeen.

A thought occurred to Robecca. "Wait, if you're not
the queen, then who is?"

Draculaura's mouth fell open. She hadn't thought
about that. She wiped her eyes on the hem of a nearby
skirt. "Only the Vampire's Heart knows, and it's been
missing for…" She stopped, realizing something.
"Wait! Maybe this is how I can help! How I can finally
do something important to make a difference to my
people! If I find the Heart, I find the queen! And *she*
can put a stop to Stoker!"

"Yes!"

"Fright on, ghoul!"

"As long as you get to keep some shoes," said Cleo.

Draculaura's plan lifted her mood. There was only
one problem. "Though, uh, how am I going to do that?"

Robecca had been having such strange feelings
since she'd arrived at the castle—a tingling feeling, a
warm glow inside. She didn't think it was just being

with her friends. It was something else. "I have a strong feeling that there are clues here in the castle, but where?"

Draculaura knew at once. "Stoker's study! He went batty when he thought I was going through his stuff. I'll distract him while you all sneak in and search it."

"Great idea!" said Clawdeen, always ready for adventure. "Time to kick some bat!"

After a few minutes of hurried planning, Draculaura went searching for Lord Stoker. She bounced toward him in the hall with a mischievous smile on her face. "Hello, Stokey!" she chirped.

"It's Lord Stoker, my…queen." He sighed irritably. "Have you made your decision?"

"I have!" Draculaura was trying to be as simple as Lord Stoker thought she was. "I was hoping to go over some questions about the whole being queen part… thing." She batted her eyelashes.

Lord Stoker rolled his eyes. He didn't like having visitors in his castle. "Ask if you must, but make it quick. You have an appointment with important vampbassadors."

"Oooh," squealed Draculaura. "This won't take… uh…too long." She winked at Clawdeen, Robecca, and Cleo as they sneaked by.

Draculaura explained to Lord Stoker that she wanted to learn how to wave properly. She dragged him into the throne room, which was across the castle from his study. "Okay, just look," she said, dragging out each word. "Should I wave with my left arm? Or with my right arm?"

Lord Stoker was impatient. "It does not matter."

"Okay, okay!" bubbled Draculaura. "Then I'll do right. How does that look?" She pranced up to the throne, practicing waves. "Now, do you want me to wave from the elbow or the wrist? Because I was thinking I could do a fun combination of jazz hands...."

Lord Stoker threw up his hands in frustration. "Wave however you please! We have no time for this. I must present a queen to the vampbassadors. Let us go!"

Lord Stoker turned on his heel to exit the throne room.

"Okay," drawled Draculaura with careful

calculation. "I guess I don't have to be that convincing of a queen for the vampbassadors. Who cares if they think I look fake?"

Lord Stoker slowly turned around to face Draculaura. Across the long expanse of the throne room, he glared at her. Was she threatening him? But no, she couldn't be. She wasn't clever enough. "Ah. I suppose a little more preparation could not hurt," he said.

Draculaura grinned. "Oh, great! That will be fangtastic! Okay, let's pick out a coronation outfit. I like pink. It's my favorite color—what's yours?"

Lord Stoker has one week to find the next vampire queen . . . or else.

All hail the
new queen!

The ghouls arrive at Castle Dracool.

Clawdeen reviews a clue that leads to more adventures.

Clawdia and Honey Swamp team up behind the scenes.

HAUNTLYWOOD

"Frights, frights, frights, Hauntlywood is in our sights!"

Draculaura pleads with Veronica to help her!

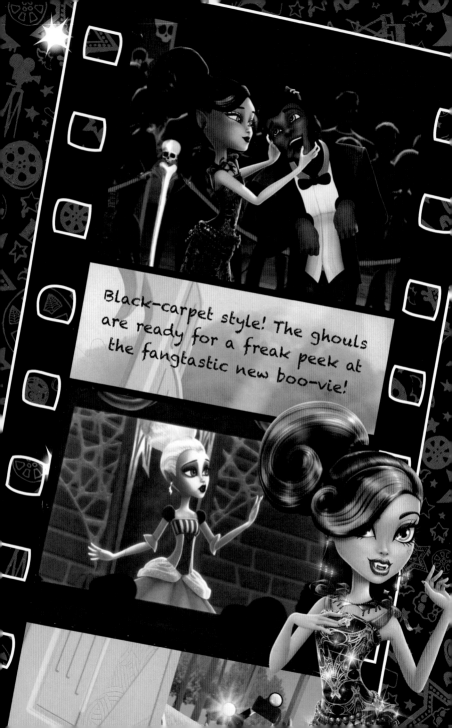

Black-carpet style! The ghouls are ready for a freak peek at the fangtastic new boo-vie!

CHAPTER 9

FRIGHT FLIGHT

Ygor was guarding the door to Lord Stoker's study and trying to swat away an annoying fly. He lifted his short leg and tried to execute a jujitsu move at the fly—and ended up flaof his life being confused.

The ghouls were spying on him from around the corner.

"Okay, how do we sneak in?" asked Clawdeen.

"That Ygor guy's not exactly the roundest gizmo in the gear, but he's not leaving that door."

Cleo looked around at the tapestries, paintings, and suits of armor in the hallway. "There has to be a secret passage. But where?" Now if she'd been in a pyramid, she'd have known exactly where to look, but castles were, well, so modern.

"Achoo!" A suit of armor down the hall sneezed.

"Ghoulsundheit!" said the ghouls.

The armor started laughing. Clawdeen growled

softly. Robecca took a step backward. Cleo wondered if castles had curses like pyramids.

A raggedy hand emerged from the armor and lifted the helmet. Two button eyes blinked in the candlelight. It was Hoodude!

"Did ya miss me?" he said cheerfully. He tried to wave at the girls but the armor toppled over and crashed to the floor. "I'm good! I'm good!"

Robecca rushed over to help him stand upright again. "What are you doing here?"

"I stowed away! I just couldn't wait a whole week to see all the royalty."

Clawdeen was stunned. "So you've been hiding in the armor this whole time?"

"Oh no! I've been everywhere. This place is loaded with secret passages." Hoodude clanked over to the wall and pulled one of the sconces. Immediately, a tunnel appeared in the wall. "See!"

"Whoa!" said the girls all together. For someone so goofy, Hoodude certainly seemed able to figure things out! They followed him into the darkness of the passageway.

After all kinds of twists and turns, Hoodude

revealed a hidden entrance to Lord Stoker's study—through a fake bookshelf!

"Here we are!" he announced. "Lord Grumpypants's study!" He shut the bookshelf behind the girls but accidentally caught himself in the lock. He tripped, ripped, reached up to steady himself, and pulled a painting off the wall. Sprawled on the floor of the study, he looked at the portrait. It showed a young vampire girl. Thick glasses covered her eyes, there were zits on her nose, and her fangs had braces on them. Still, she was smiling cheerfully.

"That's Elissabat." Clawdeen recognized her. "Lord Stoker's niece. The one Draculaura was telling us about. The one who disappeared."

"You sure they're related?" questioned Cleo. "I mean, that ghoul is actually smiling."

The painting fascinated Robecca for some reason she couldn't explain, and she pulled out her iCoffin to snap a photo of it. Maybe it would turn out to be a clue. She took the painting from Hoodude and placed it back on the wall, but as she did so, she noticed a dusty picture of Dracula. The famous

vampire had a
cape covering his
face except for his
eyes, which were
dark and piercing.

"Draculaura's father!" said Robecca.

"Whoa, lemme see!" Hoodude clambered to his
feet, tripping again and knocking the picture to the
ground. The picture flew across the room and landed,
upside down, on the floor.

The ghouls gasped. Stuck to the back of the frame
was a letter with a wax seal.

"Neato!" Hoodude exclaimed.

While the ghouls were wondering what to do, he
grabbed the letter, ripped the seal, and opened it. He
was just about to start reading it when Clawdeen took
it out of his hand.

She settled into a chair. "*Dear Count Dracula…
As my father's beast friend, I beseech you…I have
discovered that I am the next heir in line to be the
vampire queen. If my uncle finds out, he will use me to
control all vampires to ensure our supremacy over other
monsters.*"

Clawdeen lowered the letter and met the amazed
expressions of the other ghouls. This was more than a
clue. This was *the* clue, the explanation for everything.
She continued reading. "*I do not want to be a puppet,*

but Lord Stoker is too strong and I am too young and weak to stand up to him, so I must flee."

As Clawdeen read, all the ghouls could picture the vampire girl in the picture writing these words. She probably wrote the letter at this very desk, sealed it right where they were standing, and hid it behind the portrait. It gave them chills.

"*Since the Vampire's Heart is the only way to find me, I must take it,*" read Clawdeen. "*I can only trust you, Count Dracula, to be its new guardian until another queen arises.*"

She must have used the secret passageway to escape from the study. The Vampire's Heart would have glowed in her hands as she snuck away. "*Meet me in the Fog of Doom, where the Globe meets the Tower,*" finished Clawdeen, "*and I will leave another note for you in the crown. Elissabat.*"

The girls could just imagine Lord Stoker's reaction when he emerged from his coffin to find his niece gone—and the Vampire's Heart vanished.

"Wow," said Clawdeen. "Major clue. But I don't get it. Fog of Doom?"

Robecca went over to the bookshelf, the real one, and pulled out an atlas. She opened to a map of Londoom and placed it on the desk.

"Here," she said, pointing. "But I don't see anything about a crown."

"Scootch over, ghoul," said Cleo, pushing her aside. "Crowns are my department. It's obvious she's talking about the Crown Jewels in the Tower of Londoom." Cleo pointed to the Tower, clearly labeled on the map.

Clawdeen was bursting with excitement. "C'mon, let's show this letter to Draculaura!" The ghouls rushed back to the secret passageway. In their excitement, they left the atlas open on Lord Stoker's desk.

The ghouls reemerged in the hallway just in time to see Draculaura coming around the corner with Lord Stoker. They ducked into the girls' bathroom.

"Um, girls' bathroom. B-R-B, Lord Stoker," said Draculaura, who'd seen where her friends had gone.

"Make it quick!" he ordered.

"What did you find?" Draculaura asked the moment the door was closed behind her.

"Who the real queen is!" Clawdeen handed Draculaura the letter.

Robecca couldn't keep the secret. "Elissabat!" she said.

Draculaura leaned against the cold stones of the wall to steady herself. "My old friend? No…" How amazing was that?

"Yes," confirmed Cleo. "And we know where she went!"

"Londoom!" Robecca revealed.

This was so much for Draculaura to take in. How were they going to get to Londoom without Lord Stoker finding out?

But Clawdeen had already thought about this. She came from an enormous litter of pups with brothers and sisters all over the world. "My older sister Clawdia is studying dramatic writing there! She knows Londoom like the back of her paw!"

Outside in the hallway, the ghouls could hear Lord Stoker stamping his feet. "Enough of this!" he shouted through the door. "The vampbassadors await. Ygor, fetch the queen!"

A moment later, there was a timid knock on the

door to the girls' bathroom. "My queen, Ygor is to take you to the vampbassadors."

The ghouls looked at each other.

"Just a sec!" yelled Draculaura.

Clawdeen tugged on the toilet flusher to try and cover the noise of their planning, but when she did so, another secret door in the wall opened—and there was Hoodude. He yelped with embarrassment when he realized where he was.

Draculaura couldn't believe her eyes. "Hoodude?"

Hoodude laughed. "Hi, Draculaura!"

Draculaura shook her head. There was no time to lose. She led her friends into the secret passageway. It was very, very dark, but Robecca's goggles lit up to show them the way.

"How do we get out of here?" asked Clawdeen.

"Below the castle, there's a dock with a boat. We can sneak out to Londoom on that!" Hoodude had thought of everything.

Ygor was waiting outside the bathroom door. He knew he was going to get in so much trouble if he was late. But what could he do? Finally, he put his hands over his eyes and charged into the bathroom. "Ah! You are coming with Ygor!"

With his eyes shut, he waved his arms around, trying to find the vampire girl. He hit his arm against the stalls, the sinks, the soap dispenser, but other than that…nothing. He risked a peek and opened one eye. All the stalls were empty. There was no one in the bathroom.

"Uh-oh!" he realized. "Master will be angry."

He lumbered to the throne room as fast as he could. The dignitaries were checking their watches and becoming increasingly impatient.

"Where is the queen, Stoker?"

"The monarchy must be restored!"

"Stoker, you didn't lie to us, did you? Because you can be replaced."

Ygor whispered to Stoker, whose face became whiter and whiter.

"Uh, just a moment," he said to the dignitaries through gritted fangs. "The queen has had a…makeup malfunction. Please. Wait here."

Dragging Ygor behind him, he hurried out of the throne room to see if he could find Draculaura.

But Draculaura and her ghoulfriends were boarding a boat to Londoom! Hoodude had led them down the dank passageway to a dock at the edge of the river. Water lapped against the pier.

"Ta-dah!" Hoodude said triumphantly. He pointed at a small rowboat.

"Ugh," spat Cleo. "It'll take us a century to get to Londoom in that old thing."

But Robecca had an idea. She hopped into the boat and put her feet over the edge into the water. She was wearing rocket boots after all—and there was no reason they wouldn't work as propellers! "How about a steamship?" She smiled.

She let loose a blast of steam and the boat sped around in a circle, sending a wave splashing up across the dock.

"Cool!" said Clawdeen.

"All aboard the SS *Robecca*!" Draculaura giggled.

"It's not first class, but it'll do." Cleo sighed.

The ghouls clambered into the rowboat.

"Our very own royal vampire adventure!" exclaimed Hoodude. "Oh, I'm just like Veronica von Vamp! Except I'm a boy. And not a vampire. And no one's fighting over me...."

Clawdeen was hanging over the prow of the boat, the wind in her hair. "Can't you make this thing go any faster?"

Robecca went full throttle and the boat took off through the water, throwing Hoodude into the back of the boat.

"Whoa!" he yelled. This was going to be some trip!

CHAPTER 10

WHO'S THE SCARE-EST OF THEM ALL?

Back at Monster High, *everyone* was talking about vampires. Either they were talking about the coronation and what they were going to wear or they were talking about Veronica von Vamp's boo-vie and which vampire was the hottest. It was all getting mixed up in people's minds so that some of the ghouls had become convinced that Draculaura was the one who had to choose between Edweird and Alucard.

The biggest question in the Creepateria was who was cuter. Howleen smoothed a pink strand of hair back into place and sighed. "Only four days until the coronation. I hope I get to meet a vampire prince like Alucard. He is monstrously hot!" She smooched a glossy fan photo.

Toralei, who was walking by with her werecats, overheard this and hissed. "Hot? So not. The cute one is Prince Edweird, duh." She picked up her milk carton and tipped it over the photo of Alucard.

"Hey!" howled Howleen.

Toralei bared her claws and teeth.

From a nearby table, Gil and Deuce couldn't figure out what the fuss was about. "Why are they arguing?" said Gil. "I can't even tell those dudes apart."

In another corner of the Creepateria, Frankie, Lagoona, and Abbey were clustered around Ghoulia's laptop. They were video chatting with Draculaura, who was explaining to her friends everything that had happened since they'd left for Transylvania.

"And here's a picture of Elissabat. Thanks for the web search, Ghoulia. In the meantime, we're on the way to Londoom! Laters!"

"Laters!" said Frankie, Lagoona, and Abbey, crowding into the screen.

The image clicked off and Ghoulia shut the computer.

Frankie was trying to take it all in. "Draculaura isn't queen, which is bad for her, but she gets to come back to Monster High, which is good for us. I don't know how I feel about this."

Ghoulia grunted.

"I don't think so, Ghoulia," said Lagoona. Like all the other ghouls, she was fluent in Zombie. "It's better if people don't know Draculaura's looking for the Vampire's Heart...or Elissabat."

"Ohh! Y'all know I don't like secrets," drawled Operetta.

The ghouls spun around to see the phantom girl leaning against the wall. She'd overheard everything they'd said!

✗ ✗ ✗ ✗ ✗

"Unless I'm in on them," Operetta added. She pulled up a chair. "Whatcha got?"

Now if only the ghouls could keep everyone else at Monster High from finding out Draculaura's secret!

CHAPTER 11

WEREWOLVES OF LONDOOM

A foghorn boomed, bells chimed, and a speedboat whirred toward the docks of Londoom. Robecca cut the power of her rocket boots and the boat glided to a perfect stop. The girls stepped out carefully, looking around. Almost the first thing they saw was a poster for the new Veronica von Vamp boo-vie.

"Ugh!" Draculaura sighed. "We can't seem to get away from her."

Hoodude, however, was thrilled to see *any* picture of his idol. "Ooooooh! They're making a sequel to *Vampire Majesty*," he noted.

Robecca knew how this would upset Draculaura. "We are on a quest for real vampire royalty."

"Yeah," agreed Draculaura, "not some Hauntlywood phony who doesn't know a *thing* about vampire scaritage." She smiled at Robecca, grateful for her understanding.

But something intrigued Robecca about the poster. Even after the others had headed to the street, she was still staring at it. There was a clue there, she was sure of it, but she didn't know what.

"Robecca, c'mon," Clawdeen called.

"Oh, uh, sorry! Coming!" She took one last look at the poster and ran to join the others.

Clawdeen texted her sister and let her know they were on their way. They had agreed to meet at the plaza in front of the Globe Theater, right by the statue of William Spooksfear. The famous playwright was holding a skull in his hand.

"Cool statue!" noted Hoodude. "This must be the first ventriloquist act ever!"

"That's no dummy! That's William Spooksfear," said Clawdia, emerging from behind the statue. "For four hundred years, he's been inspiring actors, directors, and writers."

Like her sister, Clawdia had a bountiful mane of curls. She was dressed in the height of Londoom fashion with a red couture jacket

and a tight printed gold-
and-black dress. The glasses
she wore were the one sign
that she was a writer.

"Clawdia!" exclaimed
Clawdeen, wrapping her sister
in a hug. "Thanks, big sis, for helping."

"Sure! We Wolves are known for our loyalty,"
she said. "C'mon, you're just in time for the tour."
She led the ghouls through the fog toward the heart
of the city—and the Tower of Londoom.

There wasn't much time to lose. Back in
Transylvania, Lord Stoker had discovered the
open atlas on his desk—and knew the ghouls were
headed to Londoom. He ordered Ygor to find

Draculaura and bring
her back. There was no
way he could have her
flapping her fangs about
the Vampire's Heart. If
she did, his reign of power
would be over.

At the Tower of
Londoom, a pair of sleepy zombies guarded the
Jewel Room. They were snoring peacefully, as
were the crows resting on their shoulders. The
ghouls easily slipped by them.

"There's the crown!" said
Clawdia, pointing at a display.

Cleo wasn't impressed. "Where are the scarabs?"

The other ghouls also thought it was pretty
ordinary.

"I don't see any clues," said Draculaura,
disappointed.

"We're going to need to take a closer look,"
Clawdeen suggested. "I have an idea, but it's tricky."

Clawdeen told her sister to wake up the guards
and say that she had a thorn in her paw. Meanwhile,
Robecca would let out a burst of steam to cover.

"And what do I do?" asked Hoodude.

The girls gasped when they saw him. He had the
crown on his head!

That was the moment,
of course, when the zombie
guards awoke.

"That bloke is stealing
the crown jewels!" yacked
one of the crows.

The zombies groaned,
coming to life.

"Hoodude!" screamed the girls in a fit of panic.

Zombies moaned, crows cawed, and the ghouls were screaming. They ran down a hallway in the Tower, the guards after them. The crown fell off Hoodude's head and Clawdia caught it.

"There's no clue on this," she said, examining it as she ran.

Draculaura stopped to look at it and realized Clawdia was right. But the zombies were lurching around the corner.

"Here you go!" said Clawdia. She tossed them the crown.

The zombies and the crows crashed into one another in their hurry to retrieve the stolen jewels.

"Sorry, guys. He thought it was a souvenir." Clawdia turned to Hoodude and pretended to scold him. "I told you the gift shop is downstairs. Silly boy!"

The zombies moaned angrily, but with the crown back in their hands, they turned around and disappeared.

The ghouls were relieved—except for Robecca. "This doesn't spin right. I could feel that we were on the right track."

The others didn't have any idea what she was talking about. "What exactly was the clue?" Clawdia asked thoughtfully. Clawdeen pulled out Elissabat's letter to reread it. *"Where the Globe meets the Tower, and I will leave another note for you in the crown..."*

Clawdia's eyes lit up. "Oooh! Elissabat's not talking about the crown jewels." She walked over to a window and pointed back toward the theater where they had all originally met. "She means *that* crown. Back at the Globe Theater."

Without another word, the ghouls dashed back the way they had come. There wasn't a moment to lose.

They raced across Londoom to the Spooksfear statue holding the skull.

"A crown," explained Clawdia, the writer, "can also mean the top of the head. Or, more relevantly, a skull."

Cleo shivered. "I think I like the regular kind of crowns better."

Robecca was continuing to act very strangely. She seemed distracted. "I can't explain this, but I feel like I've been here before...." On instinct, she went up to the statue and began running her hands over the skull. A moment later, the skull was opening up—and revealing a hidden parchment!

"Wow!" said everyone.

Clawdeen reached for the parchment. It was a map with another note and more clues.

"Yeah!" shouted the ghouls, relieved.

"*Count Dracula,*" read Clawdeen. "*It is too dangerous here. I, Elissabat, am taking the*

Heart and fleeing to the Boo World. Here is a map of my destination."

Draculaura studied the map. "New Goreleans! My father took me there when I was just a little ghoul."

"And that's where my father lived when I was under construction," said Robecca.

"She must have taken the Heart there," Cleo guessed.

"We have to go find it!" said Draculaura.

"Next stop, New Goreleans!" added Clawdeen.

"And I'm going with ya," said Clawdia, surprising the ghouls. "Mom and Dad would shed fur if I didn't keep an eye on you ghouls. Besides, this will make a great story someday...and I'm gonna write it!"

Within moments, the ghouls and Hoodude were back on the boat and steaming across the ocean with Robecca's help. Paddling along behind them, frantically trying to catch up, was Ygor.

CHAPTER 12

FANGMAN STYLE

While the ghouls were on the hunt for the true vampire queen, everyone back at Monster High was fighting over the cutest vampire boo-vie star.

Toralei held up a fan photo of the vamp hottie. "Roaw! Whatevs, fleabag. Edweird is cuter."

"As if, litter lover—you can't see the obvious awesomeness of Alucard? It's right in front of your face!" Howleen brandished her own picture.

Frankie nodded in agreement. "Totally!"

Howleen smiled triumphantly at Toralei, as if Frankie had settled everything. "See? Everybody likes Alucard."

Lagoona and her boyfriend, Gil, had come over to see what all the fuss was about. "Sorry," said Lagoona. "I'm on Team Edweird. There's just something special there that Alucard doesn't have."

"I don't even know which one you're talking about," said Gil, confused.

"How about you, Twyla?" Howleen and Toralei cornered the shy boogie girl.

"C'mon, looks don't make the monster. I can't just crush on a shadow I've only seen on the silver scream. I mean, it's what's in his heart that counts. You can't judge a bat by its wings, right?"

Toralei stared at Twyla, dumbfounded. "Okay, officially ignoring you," she said finally. "Anyway, Edweird is purrrrrr-fect!"

More ghouls joined the discussion—with some arguing for Edweird and others for Alucard.

"Edweird is perfect!"

"He makes a splash!"

"Rock solid!" said Rochelle the gargoyle.

Twyla rolled her eyes as the Alucard supporters insisted he was cuter, sweeter, and hotter.

All the ghouls had been ignoring the one real boy in their midst, who had been studying the posters of both boo-vie stars.

"No one thinks they look exactly alike?" Gil asked. But he might as well have been talking underwater for all the attention anyone paid him.

CHAPTER 13

BOO ON THE BAYOU

A skeleton band marched down the streets of New Goreleans, filling the steamy city with the sounds of jazz. All kinds of monsters were dancing to the music. Someone threw beads down from a balcony.

"Now these monsters know how to party!" Hoodude joined right in, flopping his arms to the lively music.

But the ghouls didn't have time to dance; they had to find the next clue. As they rushed down the street, Hoodude saw another poster for the Veronica von Vamp movie and blew it a kiss. "Muah!"

Out of breath and exhausted, Ygor arrived at the docks of New Goreleans just in time to see the ghouls disappearing around the corner. He pulled out his iCoffin and called Lord Stoker.

The vampire's voice blared. "If they locate the Vampire's Heart, then they can find the rightful queen. We cannot let that happen. You know what to do."

"Yes, Master, I won't let you down," panted Ygor. And with that he dropped his iCoffin in the water.

"Ygor? Ygor?" came Lord Stoker's voice from underwater.

"Sorry, Master," said Ygor as he fished around and brought it up dripping.

The ghouls were headed to a dank swamp. Green moss hung from the trees. Mist hung low on the water. There were no buildings here, no statues—and no clues.

"There's nothing here. Maybe this old map is out of date," suggested Clawdeen.

"No," said Robecca. "The answer is here. I can feel it."

"I think somebody needs to have their gears checked," said Cleo.

Hoodude was the first to notice the swamp water

beginning to ripple. The clouds cleared and a shaft of moonlight fell on an enormous ghost ship quietly sliding up the bayou.

"Awesome, right?" said Draculaura.

"All right, yeah!" agreed the ghouls. Now *this* was a clue.

The ghostly steamboat came to a standstill right near them. The girls headed up a ramp to explore the old ship. Tinkly piano music wafted through the air as they entered an old theater.

"Oh my Ra!" said Cleo, admiring the cobwebs.

"Absolutely fabulous," agreed Clawdeen.

"Gore-geous!" said Draculaura.

"What is this place?" asked Hoodude.

"I've read about this ship," said Clawdia. "It was a floating theater called *The Bijou on the Bayou*. Check out all the old props and scripts." She gestured near the stage, where boxes were filled with theatrical materials covered in dust.

As if on cue, phantom skeletons tap-danced onto the stage, their bones rattling and shaking in time to the haunted music.

"Oh yeah!" cheered Hoodude, joining in.

The ghostly show helped Draculaura realize something. "You know, every place Elissabat tried to meet with my dad had to do with a theater...."

Hoodude spinning around interrupted her words—he had just seen the glowing red eyes of some strange creature slithering onto the deck.

"Uh, ghouls, I think you should look at this...." His voice was trembling.

Cleo was annoyed. "We don't have time to watch your dance— Ahhh!" She had seen the eyes too!

"Ahhhh!" All the ghouls screamed in terror, except for Draculaura.

"What is it?" she wondered.

Emerging from the shadows was an elegant blue-hued swamp ghoul with a tiny pink

hat jauntily tipped on her mass of curls. She spoke in the soft drawl of an aristocrat. "Sweet suffering swamp moss! Hey, y'all are in my shot!" She pointed at her video camera with its two glowing red lights.

"Who are you?" asked Draculaura.

"I'm Honey Swamp. Pleased to make y'all's acquaintance."

"What are you doing here?" Clawdeen was amazed that there was a ghoul just like them out on this lonely, haunted steamboat.

"I'm making my student film," explained Honey, "about the famous *Bijou on the Bayou* theater."

Draculaura realized at once how helpful their new friend might be. "We're looking for an ancient valuable artifact. Do you think it might be on the *Bijou*?"

Honey held up her camera, panning around the theater. "Well, so many great actors, writers, and directors have toured through here. Ya know, the boo-vie star Veronica von Vamp gave her first performance here! Ain't she a peach?"

"Oh yes!" agreed Hoodude, jumping off the stage.

Draculaura rolled her eyes. "No. Not a fan."

The boat lurched and the ghouls went sprawling across the room. The steamboat was moving! They could hear its enormous paddle wheel churning the water. The boat had broken away from the ramp and there was no way to get off. What was happening? They scrambled out of the theater only to see Ygor up in the bridge. He was going to drive the boat back to Transylvania!

"Oh no!" wailed Draculaura. "We can't go back without the Heart!"

Ygor was talking on his iCoffin. "Ygor good! Ygor bring the ghouls to Master."

Honey Swamp winked. "Don't worry, ghouls. I got friends in low places." She whistled and the eyes

of monster alligators appeared in
the water. They lifted their backs and made a perfect
bridge from the boat to the shore.

"C'mon!" invited Honey. "Y'all go first. I wanna
catch this on film!"

The ghouls leaped across the bumpy green backs
of the alligators while Honey kneeled down to get the
right angle with her camera and track the action.

"Cut!" she yelled just as she too leaped to shore.

The voice of Lord Stoker could be heard screaming
through Ygor's iCoffin. "Ygor, you brainless lunk! Stop
them!"

"Yes, Master!"

But Ygor had taken his hands off the steering
wheel, and the boat plowed into the riverbank. Ygor
was hurled into the air like a ball and landed in the
swamp with a splash. Slowly, the boat began to sink,
and the alligators, no longer needed as a bridge,
flicked their tails and turned toward the juicy monster

bobbing in the water. "Ah!" screamed Ygor, swimming as fast as he could toward land.

Draculaura watched the boat go down. "I'm sorry about *the Bijou on the Bayou*," she said to Honey.

"Oh, it ain't nothing to worry about, y'all. It's a ghost ship. It'll rise again on the next full moon."

Clawdeen threw up her paws. "So we have to wait a whole month to find out if the Vampire's Heart was even on the ship?" The girls were heading back along the road toward New Goreleans.

"Didn't anyone see anything remotely resembling a clue?" asked Cleo.

All that remained of the ship were a few bubbles on the surface of the water. What were they going to do?

"Whoa!" drawled Honey Swamp. "Hold on there. Let's rewind. I took some amazing shots of *the Bijou on the Bayou*. Let's check my footage!"

The ghouls crowded around the camera's view screen and Honey pressed play. Nothing jumped out at them as being a clue—until Draculaura spotted a painting on the wall of the theater. Honey Swamp rewound the tape and zoomed in.

"There!" screamed Draculaura. "That wax seal. It's Elissabat's!"

Robecca lowered her goggles to magnify the image. "*Lord Dracula,*" she read, "*as long as I have the Vampire's Heart, its glow will lead others to me. I cannot wait any longer, so I am steaming onward. I have found someone we both trust, an eternal friend, and given to their care…the Vampire's Heart.*"

"The Heart could be anywhere." Draculaura sighed, frustrated. "This is a wild-ghost chase. I can't stop Lord Stoker. So much for helping vampirekind."

"Wait a minute," said Clawdia. "In literature, everything has a reason, a purpose. Nothing is coincidental. If I were writing this, I would use a literary device. Foreshadowing or symbolism perhaps—"

"Or," interrupted Robecca, "what about just putting it on a poster?"

"Well, not super subtle, but I guess if it served the story.…" said Clawdia.

"No, there!" She pointed to a

half-rolled poster stuck to a nearby building. "Veronica von Vamp!" Robecca went over and unfurled the bottom of the poster—revealing Veronica von Vamp holding the Vampire's Heart.

"Whoa!"

"Cool!"

"The Vampire's Heart! In the boo-vie?"

Robecca was totes revved! "My wheels are clicking. Elissabat must have given the Heart to Veronica. They were both here in New Goreleans at the same time."

Draculaura was confused. "Why would my dad trust that vamp-poseur Veronica?"

Clawdia looked thoughtful. "One way to find out. I do believe Honey Swamp and I are thinking the same thing."

Honey Swamp grinned. "Time to take this story to…"

"Hauntlywood!" chimed in Clawdia.

"Yeah! Let's go!" agreed all the ghouls, excited.

Ygor heaved himself down the street in his heavy, wet clothes just in time to hear the word *Hauntlywood* and the ghouls' laughter.

"Hauntlywood, here we come!" sang out Cleo. The girls linked arms and got ready to travel again.

CHAPTER 14

BACK BITES

The Creepateria was buzzing with the news of the ghouls' Hauntlywood adventure. Ghoulia had just shared a message that had come through on her laptop. Frankie was amazed that they'd traveled so far and Lagoona was wondering what stars they'd see.

Of course, at the very mention of Hauntlywood, Howleen couldn't stop talking about Alucard and Toralei started yowling Edweird's name.

Abbey couldn't have been less interested in their fight. "Ghoulia is right. This *which boy is cuter argument* is totes cray-cray."

"We'd better do something or it's the Ghostfields and McFangs all over again!" Operetta pointed out.

Howleen was roaring and Toralei was hissing. Back and forth. Their fangs and claws were out.

None of the guys could figure out what the fuss was about.

Gil shook his aquarium-covered head. "Don't they seem the same to you guys?"

"Can't tell them apart," admitted Clawd, chewing on a leftover bone.

"Just a couple of dudes," said Deuce.

"How dare you compare Alucard to Edweird? He looks like he has bat breath," shrieked Toralei.

Howleen pounced. "Those are fighting words!"

Suddenly a high note pierced the roar in the Creepateria. Windows shattered from the sound. Everyone froze. There, standing atop the chandelier, her mouth wide open, was Operetta.

She cleared her throat. "Now that I have your attention, I gotta say, this has gone too far."

Abbey stood up. "Yeah, cool it."

"Now, back in Gnarlston," said Operetta, "we solve our differences by having a good old-fashioned trial."

The monsters exchanged glances. What was she talking about?

Operetta grinned. "We are going to settle this in... Cute Court!"

CHAPTER 15

HOORAY FOR HAUNTLYWOOD!

A bus roared down Mull-Horror Drive in Hauntly-wood. The ghouls peered out of the window. Sure, there were clues to find—but there were also sights to see!

"Hauntlywood, get ready to meet Monster High!" announced Clawdeen with a howl.

"C'mon! Let's find that star that leads to the queen of the silver scream," said Draculaura.

"And...*action!*" Honey Swamp was going to film the whole trip.

First stop was the ocean. The ghouls linked hands and started singing together. "*Frights, frights, frights, Hauntlywood is in our sights! Frights, frights, frights, Hauntlywood is in our sights! Where my ghouls at? Hey! Hey! Hey!*"

They were so caught up in the excitement that they didn't see Ygor following them—and falling off the pier into the water!

Next they visited the famous Hauntlywood sign on the hill. The ghouls were still singing! *"Freaky fangtastic, looks we got 'em. So skulltastic, feeling claw-some! So much fun, the ghoulest fashions, here we come…Frights, camera, action!"*

Ygor caught up with them just in time to see them snapping and posting a photo for their friends. Ducking out of the way, he crashed off a letter into the hillside.

At Groaning's Theater, the ghouls pretended to put their own stars in the cement. Then it was time to visit a boo-vie studio—and see if they could find Veronica von Vamp.

A large security gargoyle, so enormous his tight uniform barely covered his bloated body, was sitting by the security gate.

"Hello," said Clawdeen, who was always friendly with strangers. "We're looking for Veronica von Vamp."

"Name?" asked the gargoyle.

Hoodude shook his head. He didn't think he could wait another minute to see his favorite boo-vie star. "We just told you. Veronica von—"

"No, ya big pincushion, *your* name."

"Oh!" Hoodude chuckled. "Hoodude Voodoo."

The gargoyle looked down at his clipboard. "Nope, not on the list. Thanks for stoppin' by. Buh-bye."

The ghouls were crushed—all except for Cleo. "Ha! I got this," she said with a wink. She marched right up to the security gargoyle.

"Name?" he asked.

Cleo stared at him. "No," she said regally. "You give me *your* name, because I am Cleo de Nile!"

The gargoyle leaped to attention.

"That's de Nile as in *the* de Niles," continued Cleo haughtily. "One call to my father and I'll have you transferred to the night shift in Frightberia for the next one hundred years…if you don't open that gate this instant!"

"Um, y-yes, ma'am, I mean…uh…Miss de Nile!" stuttered the gargoyle. "Right away…here you go!"

Honey Swamp nodded. "I am impressed."

"Yeah, being a diva is, like, Cleo's superpower," whispered Draculaura.

The movie studio was bustling with showbiz star power. Actors hurried past with scripts in their hands. Crews were carrying scenery and costumes. Directors were shouting orders.

"Okay, ghouls, it's a big lot," said Clawdia. "Let's try to find Veronica fast before—"

"Anybody realizes we don't belong here?" finished Honey Swamp.

"Exactly," said Clawdia.

It was as if they could sense Ygor lurking just behind the gate, frantically putting in a call to Lord Stoker on his brand-new iCoffin.

Lord Stoker's voice was loud and furious. "Hauntlywood? Why would the Heart be in that den of mediocrity? No decent vampire would dare take it to such a place."

As usual, Ygor was out of breath. "I heard…the…*Vampire Majesty* movie…is claw-some! I would really like to see my first boo-vie if you would—"

"I will fly out immediately," came the answer on the other end of the phone. "Then we will bring Draculaura back to be my puppet queen, and I shall remain in charge forever."

Meanwhile, the ghouls were starstruck. The famous director Scare-antino was hurrying down an alley, framing shots with his fingers. He was wearing an old-fashioned black suit with a bow tie. Out of his back stuck a mechanical wind-up key.

"O-M-Ghoul!" shrieked Clawdia.

Just then, Viperine Gorgon, her snake hair flying backward as she ran in the other direction, collided with Scare-antino.

"Watch out!" yelled Draculaura, a moment too late.

Viperine's makeup kit went flying and Scare-antino's wind-up key skipped a gear and popped out. With a twitch, he started winding down. He moaned dramatically as he collapsed.

"Oh, Mr. Scare-antino! I wasn't looking," apologized Viperine. She grabbed the wind-up key and stuck it back into place.

"Gear me, I'm fading to black," he said with his last breath.

"Let me wind that for you." With a few quick twists from Viperine, Scare-antino was recharged and on the go again at top speed.

"Opening shot! Zombies to the left! Zombies to the right! Cue the music! Enter the hero! But who? Hmmm, gotta dig up some old star and resurrect his career! Note to self, pack a shovel!" He disappeared, talking a mile a minute.

Viperine began collecting her brushes and bottles from the sidewalk. "Oh no, I can't be late again." She sighed. "I'll get fired from the boo-vie for sure!"

All at once, helping hands and paws surrounded her.

"I got your scare-spray right here," said Honey. The other ghouls collected lipsticks and mascara wands.

"Thank you so much! I am Viperine. I owe you guys big-time!"

Viperine hugged Draculaura and hurried off with her makeup kit. The ghouls all had the same thought—maybe she could help them find Veronica von Vamp!

CHAPTER 16

TEAM ALUCARD VERSUS TEAM EDWEIRD

The tables in the Creepateria at Monster High had been rearranged to look like a courtroom. Toralei and Howleen sat at opposite sides, and each held in her hands a glossy photo of her vampire hottie. Ghoulia was serving as court stenographer with her laptop. Manny Taur, as the bailiff, instructed everyone to rise as the Honorable Judge Twyla, her shadowy figure cloaked in robes, entered the room.

Twyla sat down and banged her gavel.

"Cute Court is now in session," announced Spectra. "Each side will make a case for her hunk."

Howleen jumped up. "Your Honor, Alucard's adorable face and great smile make him clearly the cuter monster." She sat down, satisfied with her argument.

Toralei scoffed. "If you want a purrrfect face, you just have to look at Edweird. Pale skin. Blue eyes."

"Objection!" snarled Howleen. "The boo-vie is black and white. You don't know what color his eyes are."

"And you wouldn't know cute if it bit you on the neck!" hissed Toralei.

The court erupted into squabbling.

"Alucard is the cute one!"

"Alucard has an overbite!"

"Edweird is hideous...although normally I like that in a boy!"

Twyla banged her gavel. "Order! Order!"

The boys couldn't figure out what the fuss was about.

"I still say they look the same," muttered Gil.

"Can't tell the dudes apart," agreed Clawd.

"Yeah. Dudes," added Deuce. He was almost tempted to take off his shades and turn both Toralei and Howleen into stone.

CHAPTER 17

SCREAMS COME TRUE!

The ghouls were peeking into bungalows and soundstages on the hunt for Veronica von Vamp. Two crew monsters passed by carrying a gigantic light, and Hoodude scooted across the road to avoid them—and was hit in the head by a typewriter flying out a window!

"Yaaa-oof!" yelled Hoodude, startled. "Okay, all good, I'm good," he added, just before tripping over a bucket and falling again.

A pretty gargoyle, wearing big glasses, stuck her head out the window. She flapped her wings in frustration when she saw the typewriter on the ground. "Oops, missed. Hey, could you throw that in the trash with the other typewriters? In creative frustration?"

"Sure," said Hoodude. He picked up the typewriter and tossed it into a pile of typewriters—each with a single page of paper with one sentence typed on it.

"Sorry," said the gargoyle. "Just going through a little writer's block." She tapped her hard-as-rock head.

Clawdia gasped. She recognized the gargoyle at once. She whispered to the other ghouls. "It can't be! That's Scary Stone, the most amazing screamwriter in Hauntlywood!"

Draculaura went right over to the window. "Ms. Stone, um, if you have writer's block, my friend Clawdia is a writer. She can help."

Robecca nodded in agreement. She retrieved the thrown-away typewriter and handed it to Clawdia.

Scary Stone sighed. "This new werewolf movie? It is chewing me up!"

Shyly, Clawdia started to type. After a few minutes in which no one dared speak, Clawdia handed the typewriter to Scary.

She read it and read it again. "You've changed *Wwwoooa* to *Aooww!* So authentic, so raw, so...wolfy! It's brilliant. You have got to help me with the rest of the script."

Clawdia was stunned. What should she do? "It's always been my scream to be a writer in Hauntlywood!"

"See you later!" said Draculaura encouragingly. "Write lots of words!"

"Aw, good-bye, guys. I hope you find the—"

Scary Stone had yanked her inside the bungalow!

"Go, have fun!" urged the ghouls, happy for her. They would have liked to stick around, but they knew that they didn't have much time left to find the vampire star.

The next place they looked was a studio where a boo-vie was being filmed. Monster assistants were holding moss-covered tree branches that looked like they were right from New Goreleans. Above a director's chair hovered a ghost director, Sofeara Gorepola. Near her was a normal-looking sea-monster actor, wearing a not-so-normal-looking sea-monster costume.

"Where is my camera two?" the director was complaining. "My underwater camera?"

A gargoyle in a badly fitting wet suit and swim mask flopped over to her with a camera on his shoulder. He said something, but his snorkel muffled his words.

"Really? Made of stone? That's your excuse?" Sofeara Gorepola was furious. "I can't make this boo-vie without underwater footage!"

But the gargoyles were storming out. They sank, of course, every time they went in the water.

Clawdeen walked over to the director. "Excuse me," she said. "I think I know someone who can help." She pulled over Honey Swamp.

"Go on!" urged Draculaura. "This is your scream!"

That was all the encouragement Honey needed. "Yup!" she said. "There's nobody better if you're talking 'bout a camera and a swamp. Why, I can rack a focus while changing lenses on a backtracked steadicam."

"Whoa! What does that even mean?" Draculaura whispered to the other ghouls.

Sofeara studied Honey Swamp. She looked to the door where the gargoyle in the wet suit was still standing. "All right, I'll try you out."

The gargoyle angrily threw his camera to the ground and waddled away.

But the ghouls were thrilled for their friend. "You go, ghoul!"

"And...*action!*" called Sofeara Gorepola.

Honey waved to her friends before jumping into a pool of water—camera in hand.

Sofeara Gorepola watched the film on her director's monitor. "This is great!" exclaimed the director. "Keep rolling. And...cut! Love it!"

Honey emerged from the water and waved to her friends. She had made it in Hauntlywood! "Muah!" She blew the ghouls a kiss.

Hoodude caught it and blew one back. "Muah!"

Back outside, the ghouls saw another gargoyle staggering down the street, burdened under an enormous pile of scripts. A berserk boo-vie executive was raging at him. "I'm looking for a triple threat! Where are we gonna find someone with the pure, raw talent to handle this part?"

Hoodude went right over to the executive. "You wanna triple threat? Here I *am*!" He started singing, and the gargoyle assistant was so startled that he collapsed under the scripts. A flock of bats flew out from the eaves in a panic.

"I dance!" said Hoodude. He leaped onto a nearby ladder and twirled on it, like a tap-dancing star. He dropped to his knees, jazz hands spread wide, and announced, "Ta-dah! And I act!"

The movie executive was overwhelmed. "You got the job!" he shouted, and he pulled a contract from his pocket and had Hoodude sign it on the spot.

"Even your scream came true!" Clawdeen cheered. "Nice going!"

"We'll call you when we find Veronica," said Draculaura.

As the ghouls continued their search, the gargoyle assistant returned—this time carrying a mop and bucket. He handed them to Hoodude. "In Hauntlywood, triple threat means: dust, mop, sweep."

Hoodude stared at the cleaning gear and shrugged, still happy. "Oh well, at least I'm in show biz! Cha cha cha!"

CHAPTER 18

AND THE WINNER IS...

Cute Court was hearing evidence in the Creepateria. Howleen and Toralei were glaring at each other. Giant posters of Alucard and Edweird loomed over the proceedings.

Twyla banged her gavel. "Let me get this straight," she said to Toralei. "You say dimples are better than a chiseled chin?"

Howleen leaped up, objecting. "No! Chiseled chin!"

"Dimples!" yelled Toralei.

Ghoulia was sitting on the witness stand with her laptop. Twyla turned to her. "Ghoulia, what does science say about dimples versus chiseled chins?"

Ghoulia grunted thoughtfully. She took off her glasses and cleaned them, put them on again, and peered at the posters. She took the glasses off and crossed her eyes to create a double vision—and that's when she saw it! She put her glasses back on and started typing as fast as she could.

"Wait," said Twyla, "are you telling us..."

Ghoulia moaned, confirming what Twyla thought.
She turned her laptop around for everyone to see.
There was a photo of Alucard and there was a photo of
Edweird. But then Ghoulia superimposed them, laying
one photo over the other, and they were…identical!

"They are the same actor!" said Twyla. "Digitally
composited to seem like two different boys!"

The monsters went wild!

"What an unexpected development!" shouted
Abbey.

"Unbelievable!"

"No way!" yelped Toralei.

"Did you see it?"

"It's true!"

"Twice as delicious!" said Wydowna Spider.

"Order in the court," bellowed Manny Taur.

Twyla waited until everyone was quiet before offering up her judgment. "In the case of Alucard versus Edweird, I find...that you can't judge a bat by its wings!" She banged her gavel. "Case closed!"

"Cute Court is hereby adjourned!" Manny Taur roared.

"Totally called it," said Clawd, leaning back in his chair.

"Yep, same dude," agreed Deuce.

"I knew it!" said Gil. "And they called me crazy."

Howleen and Toralei tried to make up.

"I guess dimples are cute," admitted Howleen.

"And I could see getting used to a chiseled chin," Toralei acknowledged.

Everyone else was leaving the Creepateria, but Ghoulia was still clicking away at her laptop.

"What is it, Ghoulia?" asked Operetta.

Ghoulia turned the screen toward her. Just as she had superimposed the photos of Alucard and Edweird to show that they were the same person, she had now done the same thing with Veronica von Vamp…and Elissabat!

"Could it be?" wondered Operetta.

There was no time to lose! They had to let their friends know!

CHAPTER 19

DIRECTOR'S CUT

Draculaura, Clawdeen, Robecca, and Cleo continued to roam the lot in search of the sound stage where Veronica von Vamp was filming. A crew of skeletons passed them on the street, all carrying palm trees.

Robecca stopped and touched her heart. "We're close, ghouls. I can feel it. This way."

She led them toward a studio where gargoyles were pushing in huge set pieces—rocks, boulders, trees. Draculaura had been right! Emerging behind them was Veronica von Vamp.

She was talking to her director, Mr. Scare-antino. The ghouls couldn't hear what she was saying, but Veronica von Vamp smiled at him and sailed off toward her trailer, a gigantic Airstream guarded by two gargoyle guards.

"We have to get into that trailer!" said Clawdeen.

Cleo laughed. "That'll be easy, except for those two huge bodyguards."

"Looks like you could use a hand...." It was Viperine!

"You work on this boo-vie?" asked Clawdeen.

Viperine giggled. "Thanks to you, I didn't get fired!"

"Can you help us meet Veronica?" Draculaura wanted to know.

"Leave it to me!" Viperine led the way to the trailer. The guards tried to block their way, but Viperine told them that this was her new makeup crew.

"How come so many of you?" asked the guard, suspicious.

The snakes in Viperine's hair hissed. "We have to make Miss von Vamp very very very *very* pretty for her next scene."

She marched into the trailer with the ghouls following her. It was luxurious, with an elaborate makeup chair and a mirror framed by lights. Glossy photos of Veronica covered the walls.

"She's not here," noted Viperine.

Cleo headed over to a table covered in delicious-looking refreshments. "Then I guess we'll wait. A trailer this classy shouldn't be wasted."

"No!" exclaimed Draculaura. "I can't rest until we find her!"

The makeup chair spun around and sitting in it was…Veronica von Vamp. She raised an eyebrow. "Do I know you?"

The ghouls froze. Were they in trouble?

That's when Clawdeen saw it. "The Vampire's Heart!" She pointed at the makeup table.

"It's here!" Cleo was ecstatic.

Veronica von Vamp laughed. "Sorry, you're looking at a fake. This *is* Hauntlywood. It's only a prop."

Draculaura was disappointed—but not surprised. "We're very sorry for intruding like this, but—"

"I can always sign an autograph for a fan," Veronica von Vamp interrupted.

"Sorry," said Draculaura. "Not...umm...actually a fan. In fact, I think your stereotypical portrayal—"

Clawdeen began coughing. "Not the time!"

Viperine started doing Veronica's makeup, her snakes putting on her blush.

"Why are you looking for it?" asked Veronica, curious. She was studying Draculaura. The fact that she wasn't a fan intrigued her.

"The heart will lead us to Elissabat," explained Draculaura. "The rightful queen of the vampires."

Veronica caught her breath. "Wow, I haven't heard that name in a long time."

Everything rushed out of Draculaura. "The vampires need a queen. Quickly. And Lord Stoker chose me, but then I found out that his Vampire's Heart was a fake, so I decided to find the real one so it could lead to the real queen, who is, in reality, Elissabat!" She stopped to take a breath. "I need help."

Veronica von Vamp swiveled around in her

makeup chair. "What if she doesn't want to be the queen?"

"Everything we stand for will be undone if Stoker rules. The vampires need her," Draculaura said passionately. "All monsters need her."

Veronica von Vamp gazed into Draculaura's eyes. "If Elissabat were here, she would probably say that she's just one ghoul, nothing special, and maybe she doesn't think she has what's needed to be queen."

"I get that," Draculaura said solemnly. "It takes courage. Heart. And I know she has it. Listen, not all of us were meant to do great things. She should be proud that she was born to do something so amazing."

Veronica seemed flustered. "Look, I want to help, really I do. But I promised Elissabat I would keep her secret."

"Then you can tell her, from Draculaura—and this is big—that she ran away once, but I will find her, and that...that...I will never give up."

"Why?"

Draculaura's eyes filled with tears. "This is how I can help. How I can do something big. Something important. And when she's queen, she can help everybloody. This is a turning point in vampire history, and her duty calls to help monsters everywhere!" Draculaura's words gave her ghoulfriends chills. This meant so much to Draculaura.

A goblin opened the door of the trailer. "Ready on the set, Miss von Vamp."

"I must go," Veronica von Vamp said softly.

"Please, Miss von Vamp," Draculaura begged. "If you know where Elissabat is, you have to tell her…." Her voice trailed off into a sob.

"Elissabat disappeared a long time ago. I want to help…but…" Veronica left without finishing her sentence.

Clawdeen was frustrated. "Furrific. The Heart's a fake, and Veronica's not gonna help us. What are we gonna do now?"

"I'm sorry; it seemed like you were so close," said Viperine.

"Yes," said Robecca, distracted by something. "Elissabat *is* close. I can sense it."

"Then we keep looking," said Draculaura, determined. "Come on!"

They weren't sure where to go next, but as they made their way out of the studio, they passed through Veronica von Vamp's boo-vie set. Dry ice filled the air with fog. Out of the mist emerged Lord Stoker and Ygor!

Lord Stoker cackled. "I've got you, Your Highness."

Ygor laughed too, only he wasn't as frightening.

"No!" announced Draculaura.

As the smoke evaporated, Scare-antino the director found himself staring at two vampires he didn't realize were in his boo-vie. "Whoa, whoa, whoa! Is this in the script?"

A tiny gargoyle started flipping through a script in his hand and shook his head.

Lord Stoker loomed over Draculaura. "Now this is how it will be. You will return to Transylvania. You will take your place at the court. And you will obey me."

"No!" said Draculaura again. "I am so close to finding Elissabat!"

Scare-antino was filming the whole scene. "I love the gritty realism! Keep rolling!"

"Ha!" said Lord Stoker. "She is gone, and you will be queen whether you want to or—"

"I think not!" Veronica von Vamp, wearing her long gown and crown for the movie, had made her entrance. She was fangulous!

But Lord Stoker was unmoved. "I insist."

"And what gives you the authority?" asked Veronica von Vamp. She was wearing high heels that made her almost as tall as Lord Stoker.

"I am the prime monister of all the vampires!" said Lord Stoker.

Veronica von Vamp was unimpressed. "And I am Veronica von Vamp, boo-vie star. And you are in *my* studio."

Two gargoyle bodyguards stepped toward Lord Stoker.

"I protest," he said. "I have never been treated like this."

Veronica von Vamp smiled. "Well then, it is long overdue."

Lord Stoker changed tactics. "Your people need you," he whispered to Draculaura.

"No!" said Draculaura, a new kind of power in her voice. "They need the true queen. Monsters everywhere are counting on her. I am counting on her. You won't be able to boss *her* around. No way!"

"Hard to say." Lord Stoker snickered. "She's not here."

"You will not use that tone on my set," Veronica von Vamp commanded.

Draculaura pleaded with Veronica. "If you know where Elissabat is, please, please help."

Lord Stoker narrowed his eyes. "You know where—"

Veronica silenced him. "Draculaura is right. It is time. The vampires need their real queen—Elissabat."

A door to the sound stage burst open. It was Operetta and Ghoulia. Ghoulia started trying to explain what she had found out.

"Yeah!" said Clawdeen, listening to her. "Veronica is talking about Elissabat."

Ghoulia shook her head furiously. She tried again. She pulled her laptop out of her backpack to show everyone what she had discovered.

Clawdeen came over to look. "Veronica is…what? Say again?"

Scare-antino was filming everything. Everything! This was going to be the greatest vampire boo-vie ever!

Veronica held up her hands for quiet. "I remember Elissabat," she began dramatically. "More than anything, she wanted to act. Only onstage and in her imagination did she have the strength to lead. But my friend Draculaura has reminded me that you need to have courage to face your fear, to overcome it, to help others."

Draculaura was stunned. "I did?"

"Yes," said Veronica von Vamp. "This is a turning point in monster history. It is time to raise the curtain on a new act. Veronica von Vamp is, and always was…"

Scare-antino couldn't even breathe—well, he couldn't if he actually could breathe. This was so wonderful. It was Veronica's most powerful performance ever!

"That's right," said Veronica von Vamp. "I am…"

Draculaura inhaled sharply. She saw it at last. She knew who the vampire queen really was!

Veronica von Vamp pulled at her hair, which was really a wig, took out a pair of glasses from her pocket, and transformed into—Elissabat.

"What?" Lord Stoker gave a high-pitched shriek like a bat in trouble.

Ghoulia held up her laptop, revealing that Elissabat and Veronica von Vamp were the same person.

"The queen of the vampires!" Draculaura bowed her head respectfully.

"I knew she was close!" said Robecca.

"Yup," agreed Operetta. "She fooled us. Just goes to show—"

"You can't judge a bat by its wings," completed Honey Swamp.

"That's right!" Operetta smiled.

Veronica von Vamp approached Robecca. She took her hand. The moment Robecca touched the boo-vie star, her entire body began to glow. Robecca gasped. She fumbled with a service panel at her side and opened it up to reveal, hidden within the mechanism of her body, the Vampire's Heart. It pulsed softly and glowed.

"Whoa!" The ghouls were stunned.

"Augh!" Lord Stoker shriveled in defeat.

"I gave the Vampire's Heart to your father, Robecca. I wanted Hexiciah Steam to keep it safe. So he put it in the safest place of all. You. It led you ghouls to me." Gently, Veronica removed her hand and Robecca's glow faded.

Robecca could still feel the glow inside her—the glow that had been strengthening the closer they had come to Elissabat.

"Lord Stoker," said Veronica von Vamp, becoming very stern. "For your crimes against the vampire crown, you are banished from ever holding official office."

The gargoyles tightened their grip on Lord Stoker and he whimpered. Veronica instructed them to remove him.

"But I'm the boss of everything!" he cried. "Ygor!"

Ygor shuffled after his master, who was hauled out of the studio like a limp rag doll.

"Tonight is my new boo-vie premiere," Veronica said to the ghouls. "It will also be my coronation. And you are all invited."

The ghouls cheered!

Scare-antino swung onto the set from a crane, where he had been filming everything. "And...cut! That's a wrap. Off to the edit bay."

CHAPTER 20

THE MIDNIGHT PREMIERE!

Spotlights danced across the red carpet at Groaning's Theater. It was the big night, the premiere of *Vampire Majesty 4: The Vampire's Heart* and Elissabat's coronation. Cameras flashed as skelebrities emerged from their limos. Spectra Vondergeist was interviewing the vampires, the ghouls, and the monsters all decked out in their fanciest gowns and tuxes.

"This is Spectra Vondergeist blogging to you live from Hauntlywood for the premiere of Veronica von Vamp's new boo-vie!"

Scarah Screams, a telepathic banshee, held her hand to her head and sent a message to Spectra.

"I am told via telepath," she said into her microphone, "that the star is arriving now!"

There was an explosion of flashes and camera clicks as a white limo pulled up to the red carpet. Out stepped

Veronica von Vamp in a couture dress. She waved to the crowd—and then brought forward Draculaura.

Hoodude stumbled through the crowd. "Oh, Miss von Vamp, may I have your autograph?"

"I'm so flattered." She smiled. "Would you honor me by being my date?"

Hoodude nearly fainted. He couldn't believe it. "Huzzah!" he shouted, recovering, and took Veronica by the arm to escort her into the theater.

For a moment, Draculaura was at a loss. Where was her date? But Clawdeen pulled out a dog whistle and handed it to her.

Inside the theater, Clawd was getting his popcorn with Manny. He pricked up his ears. He knew that sound. "Draculaura! She's here!" He shoved past Manny, charged outside, and bounded over the velvet rope to be at her side. It had been a whole week since they'd seen each other. He wrapped her in a sloppy hug and she gave him a scratch behind his ears.

"Oh, Clawd, I missed you so much," said Draculaura. "Do you like that? Good boy! You missed your ear being scratched, didn't you?"

Clawd panted contentedly.

Far back in the crowd, Lord Stoker was weaseling his way into the theater. Finally, he managed to get to the main entrance and was just about to step over the rope—when Gory Fangtel stopped him.

"I don't think so." She chuckled. "You're not on the list."

Lord Stoker tried to charm her. "I just wanted to be the first one to congratulate Her Majesty, my niece, the queen."

"Yeah?" said Gory, unmoved. "How about when trolls fly?"

Two gargoyles appeared and Lord Stoker began backing away, tripped over a garbage can, and went sprawling.

One of the paparazzi snapped a photo of him on the ground.

"Oops!" said Ygor.

Lord Stoker growled.

"I just wanted to see the boo-vie," Ygor said sadly.

Gory Fangtel saw what had happened and lifted the rope for him to come on in. Ygor couldn't believe it.

"Claw-some!" he said as he headed to get some popcorn.

Inside the lobby, Scare-antino was presenting
Veronica with the Academy's highest award—the
Silver Claw! "Veronica, this is in recognition of your
deadication to acting!"

The crowd cheered.

"Thank you," said Veronica graciously. "You know,
I have made boo-vies about the vampire court, but
I have never revealed that I actually grew up there.
I would like to deadicate this award to the person
who made this evening possible. This is for my friend
Draculaura."

Draculaura gasped.

"Draculaura taught me that you need to think
beyond yourself," Veronica continued. "At this turning
point in vampire history, my duty calls to me, and I am
here to help monsters everywhere!"

A colony of bats swooped into the lobby. At their
center was a jeweled crown held aloft by their wings.

They hovered above Veronica and lowered the crown onto her head.

But that wasn't the only amazing thing that happened.

At the very moment Veronica was adjusting the crown on her head, a pink mist was wrapping itself around Draculaura.

"What's happening?" she wondered. Before anyone could answer her, she had turned into a bat and was flying around her friends.

Clawdeen knew exactly what had happened. "You got your vamp powers!"

"You did it!" Cleo applauded.

Ghoulia moaned her praise.

"Ghoulia's right," said Robecca. "Finding Elissabat and saving the vampires was your *big thing*."

Draculaura changed herself back into a ghoul. "Hey, what are we waiting for? The boo-vie is about to start with my favorite royal actress, Veronica von Vamp!"

Everyone poured into the theater. Clawd settled into a seat next to Draculaura, who was right up in the front row with Veronica.

Draculaura was still trying to take it all in. "So you're Elissabat playing Veronica playing all of those parts. You have to be the greatest boo-vie star ever!"

Veronica giggled. "Thanks. I can't wait to make the next sequel at Castle Dracool with my new screenwriter, cinematographer, and makeup artist." Clawdia, Honey Swamp, and Viperine all grinned at these words. Their screams were coming true!

The lights were dimming when the vampire hottie who played Alucard and Edweird strode down the aisle. Ghouls sighed and whispered and squealed. He gestured to a seat between Howleen and Toralei. "Is this seat taken?"

Unable to speak, the ghouls shook their heads.

The actor sat himself down between them.

Howleen sighed. "Look at that chin! He's sitting with me!"

"Dimples! Dimples! He's sitting with me," insisted Toralei.

The ghouls began growling and snarling at each other, but Abbey stopped all that with a freezing blast.

"Chill, ghouls," she said. "Hunk sitting with

me." She grabbed the actor by the arm and pulled him over his seat into her aisle. He didn't seem to mind—at all. Abbey was a knockout snowgirl.

"Hush, everyone!" said Operetta. "The boo-vie's starting!"

Just like the last boo-vie, this one was in black and white—except for Veronica's bloodred lips. She was giving the performance of a lifetime. "Not all of us were meant to do great things. She should be proud that she was born to do something so amazing."

"That's what I said to *her*!" Draculaura giggled in the audience.

"Shhhhh!" said the audience.

Draculaura cuddled closer to Clawd and took a handful of popcorn. She was really enjoying this movie—and it got everything right about vampire scaritage at last.

CHAPTER 21

ONE MORE SCREAM

At the studio, a goblin held up a slate for the camera. *Clap!* "Take one!"

It was Hoodudes's scream test!

Hoodude entered with a mop and tap-danced around a lamppost next to a puddle. He splashed in the puddle and spun around the lamppost, singing. *"I'm singin' in a stain! Just singing and flinging. And singing!"*

He spun so hard he flipped off the post and flew off the stage with a scream.

A few hours later, the goblin again held up his slate for the camera. "Take forty-seven." He sighed.

Hoodude was holding the fake Vampire's Heart. "There you are, my precious," he said, trying to make his voice sound evil. "No! That's not ours! We needs to gives it back. No! Get away! It's all mine!" He clutched it tight...and it broke!

"Uh-oh," said Hoodude. "I'm sorry; is it broken? Was it a real heart?"

A day later, the goblin held up the slate. "Hoodude Voodoo scream test, take seven hundred and fifty-two."

Hoodude stormed onto the set like Godzilla. He was tossing boxes as if they were buildings. He pulled a stuffed toy from a box, became distracted, and tripped. He knocked into the set and it toppled over.

He looked out at the exhausted crew. "I wasn't feeling that one. Can I do that take over again?"

It looked like it was going to be a long, long time before Hoodude won a Silver Claw!

Little, Brown and Company

Hachette Book Group
237 Park Avenue, New York, NY 10017
Visit us at lb-kids.com

Little, Brown and Company is a division of Hachette Book Group, Inc.
The Little, Brown name and logo are trademarks of Hachette Book Group, Inc.

The publisher is not responsible for websites (or their content)
that are not owned by the publisher.

First Edition: September 2014

Library of Congress Control Number: 2014943929

ISBN 978-0-316-37738-6

10 9 8 7 6 5 4 3 2 1

RRD-C

Printed in the United States of America